BOYS
south of the
MASON DIXON

ABBI
GLINES

#1 *NEW YORK TIMES* BESTSELLING AUTHOR

To my dad, his brothers, and Mama Potts.
This was inspired by all of you.
Mama Potts you would have loved this one.

BOYS

south of the

MASON DIXON

PROLOGUE

I OFTEN WONDERED if it was a common thing for a girl to fall in love at thirteen. And if it was, does that love last? Or is it just a crush? Can you even truly love that young? These thoughts kept me up at night. Why did I stay up thinking about love? Because Asher Sutton had given me a ride home and, in that moment, stolen my heart for good.

"Dixie Monroe, what are you doing walking out here by yourself? Ain't safe for a girl. You know better!" That thick, deep voice was Asher Sutton's. I'd know it anywhere. My cheeks heated and I felt silly. I didn't want to admit I had missed the bus because Emily James hid my clothes while I was changing after P.E. and I'd been left in the locker room naked. Until Coach Jones came in and found me. She had given me an extra P.E. uniform to wear home. It was too big and smelled funny, but it was something to wear, at least. I didn't want Asher to see me or smell me like this.

"I, uh, just wanted to walk," I stammered, hoping he wouldn't realize I was barefoot. There had been no extra shoes for me to wear. Walking in the grass felt fine on my feet. Luckily, it wasn't cold or wet outside, or I would've been in a fix.

"Well, that was a bad idea. Your daddy would have a fit and will if he catches wind you walked home. It's too damn long a walk. Get in this truck."

Asher Sutton's truck. It was famous. Well, at least the stories about that truck were. All girls in town wanted to experience Asher's truck. He was known as the best kisser in town and he was by far the most handsome boy I'd ever seen. I knew he'd had sex in that truck with a college girl just last week. And Asher was only sixteen.

I looked down at my shirt that was at least three sizes too big and the shorts that hung past my knees. I had wrapped the drawstring around me then tied it to keep the shorts from falling off. My bare feet were dirty and the pretty pink nail polish on my toes was now chipped. It no longer reminded me of cotton candy.

"It's okay. He won't mind. He knows I like to walk for exercise," I lied. It was the first thing I could think of. Because Asher was right. My daddy was not going to be happy about any of this. Not about the clothes, shoes, or my walking home. I was already preparing myself for him to go up to the school tomorrow and pitch a fit over this. But seeing as I had lost my shoes and clothes, I didn't see how I was going to hide this from him.

Unfortunately, Asher wasn't buying this story at all. "Not moving from here until you get in this truck, Dixie. Can't leave you out here to walk," he paused and I glanced up at him. His gaze had dropped to my feet. "Shit, girl, are you barefoot?"

I sighed. This had been humiliating to begin with. Now it was becoming a nightmare. Wasn't the first time Emily James had gone out of her way to make my life hell. I never could figure out why she hated me so much. I was a nice person. I tried really hard to get people to like me. But nothing I did or said could make Emily like me. Instead, she found ways to embarrass and humiliate me. Regularly. At least once a week. Never had it been this bad before. Because never had Asher Sutton witnessed it.

I knew he wasn't going to leave me out here now. Might as well get this over with. "Yeah, I, uh, lost those," I sounded like an idiot.

Asher frowned. He didn't seem amused. "Come on, Dix, get in the truck."

I did as I was told this time. It was another three miles to my house and my daddy was going to start worrying about me soon enough. I would never forgive Emily for this one though. I was done trying to be nice to her. She had taken it too far. I was in Asher Sutton's truck looking like an idiot and smelling worse.

"Thank you," I said not looking his way again once I was inside.

"Buckle up," he said, "then explain to me why you're wearing gym clothes that could fit me, don't have shoes on your feet and are walking home like that."

Lying was less embarrassing. But I was a terrible liar. Daddy said I stammered and turned red the moment I even tried to fib a little.

"Someone stole my clothes while I was changing after P.E. class." Just saying it made me sound like a loser. I had always been the little girl next door that Asher Sutton liked to tease. I wanted to look grown up and have boobs like Emily or my best friend Scarlet. Something to make me look older than thirteen.

"What the hell?" His tone was incredulous. As if he couldn't fathom that. I bet he couldn't. I doubt anyone had ever done anything like that to him. "How'd they take your clothes?"

This was just getting worse. I wished he'd drive faster. Admitting I didn't change in front of the other girls because my body wasn't developing like theirs yet was too much. But he wasn't going to stop asking unless I told him. "I change in one of the bathroom stalls. I had my clothes hanging over the door so they wouldn't touch the floor. When I took off my gym clothes, I hung them over the door and then—" I stopped. Telling Asher I had then taken that moment to use the toilet stuck in my throat. "I . . ." What did I say here?

"You had to pee?" he offered and I felt my face become an inferno.

I simply nodded.

"Then someone grabbed all your clothes and shoes?"

I nodded again.

"Fuck, wish I knew who did it."

I knew but I didn't say. Emily had slept with several of Asher's friends. She was tall and curvy and the older guys loved her. My house was finally in view and I wanted to leap out of the moving truck and start getting homeschooled tomorrow. Never leave my house again. Never have to look at Asher again.

"Your daddy is heading out to his truck with a concerned scowl on his face. Reckon he's coming to find you. Knew he'd be worried."

He had probably already talked to Coach Jones. He wasn't happy with the harassment I'd been dealing with this year. It had escalated. Today was the worst yet though.

"I need to stop him," I said, hoping Asher would speed up.

He honked his horn and Daddy stopped and looked our way. The relief on his face when he saw me made me feel bad. He had been worried. I should have called him from the school instead of trying to hide this. I just hated upsetting him.

"He ain't gonna be happy about this," Asher said.

"No, he ain't. Thanks for the ride," I told him and reached for the door.

"Dixie," he said my name gently.

"Yeah," I answered without looking at him again.

"Girls are mean as hell. But only because they're jealous. Whoever took your clothes didn't know you'd look just as pretty in a damn potato sack. Don't let them get to you. Don't let them change who you are."

Those words weren't the first Asher Sutton ever said directly to me in my life. But they were the most important for two reasons. I remembered them every single time Emily James did something cruel to me during that very long year. And they made me fall in love with Asher Sutton. Not because he was popular, beautiful, or the football captain. I fell in love at thirteen because a boy was kind to me.

chapter
ONE

Dixie Monroe

THE PAPER BAG was being crushed in my hand. The death grip I had on it from the moment I noticed that old blue Ford truck, slowly pulling through the caution light, was causing my hand to go numb. I wasn't ready to see that truck. Not yet. Steel hadn't warned me. Not about this he hadn't.

But then again . . . Steel may not know yet. I glanced over my shoulder to see if the truck was going to drive by, so I could breathe again. My heartbeat quickened as the truck pulled into a parking spot right outside Harrod's Pharmacy. He was getting out. It was him.

I knew I needed to look away. I didn't want him to catch me staring. Really, it was pathetic. Completely ridiculous and sad. Asher Sutton had destroyed me. I shouldn't react to him anymore, and I most definitely shouldn't care anymore that his face was still chiseled perfection and his body that of every woman's dreams.

Before I could gather my bearings, control my reaction to him, self-preservation kicked in, and I instinctively took a step out of his line of sight. His truck door swung open, long jean-clad legs stepping onto the pavement. The dark hair I used to run my fingers through was cut short, highlighting his stone cut face, the stubble covering his jaw making him appear like a dangerous angel. The flannel shirt he was wearing was faded and tightly joined across his chest. A chest I knew all too well was smooth and paneled with muscle.

"Don't go there, Dixie." Scarlet North, my best friend since middle school, whispered in my ear. Her hand clamped around my arm and she tugged me hard, enough to snap me out of my foolish stupor.

"Evil. Remember that, Dixie. That man is evil. He's more beautiful than any one male has a right to be on the planet. But he's the devil. You know that. Besides, don't forget about Steel. You're now dating Asher's little brother." Her last six words were a murmur. Only I could hear what she said.

Gossip in a small town was bad. In Malroy, Alabama, it was worse than bad. The place was a mecca of gossip. Everybody knew everything and everybody was in everyone's business. There was a very good chance, right there on Main Street, that people were peeking from their windows to see if I would look Asher's way. There had been enough talk about us in Malroy to last a lifetime and two years of Asher being away at college didn't change a thing.

"I didn't know he was coming home," I said, simply trying to slow down my heart rate from seeing Asher for the very first time in years. He didn't come home last summer. He stayed in Gainesville, Florida taking summer classes and seemed to have forgotten about Malroy.

"He's probably just here to see his momma. He'll leave soon enough, you'll see. Steel would've told you if Asher was coming home for the summer," Scarlet assured me.

I managed to nod while gripping my scrunched up paper

bag in front of me like a shield. Asher was back and I didn't know how to react. What was I supposed to expect? Would he keep pretending like I didn't exist? Could he even do that now that I was with his brother? Would Steel tell him? Would Asher care?

No, he wouldn't. I knew that all too well. Asher wouldn't care at all. He had made it very clear to the entire town that he didn't want me anymore. He didn't care who had me now. He was done with me. I went from being one half of the "golden couple" to the discarded girl who surely must've done something horrible for Asher to throw her away and never look back. It happened so quickly, it still made no sense to me.

He had been my safe harbor. I was secure in his love. I gave my innocence to Asher believing in my heart he would be my forever, my one and only. But he blindsided me by leaving me without any explanation whatsoever.

The people I thought were my friends believed it had been my fault, something unforgivable that I did, and quickly turned their backs on me. They all worshiped the football star that had singlehandedly put our town on the map, the boy who led our team to a State Championship two years in a row. He could do no wrong in their eyes. They had wasted no time taking his side. Everyone except Scarlet. She was my only true friend.

"He's a giant asshole. Full of himself. The great and mighty Sutton," she snarled his way.

I rolled my eyes and turned to look at her. "Don't act like being a Sutton boy is a bad thing. You're so in love with Brent Sutton you can't see straight," I pointed out.

She grinned, then shrugged and giggled. "Yeah, well, all Sutton boys ain't bad. Just that particular one there."

I agreed with her. The Sutton boys were a part of my life. They always had been and always would be. Our farms sat beside one another and our families remained intertwined.

The tiny diamond on my left hand sparkled in the bright sunlight as I lifted it. "No, they aren't all bad," I said. "One or two are decent enough."

Scarlet released a sigh and shook her head. "Why are you wearing that? I thought you were still thinking about it?"

I glanced back at Asher's blue truck, unable to pretend like it wasn't there. My heart twisted painfully in my chest. He still had a crazy hold over me, and no amount of pep talk could do anything about it. "I wanted to see how it felt," I admitted shyly, before glancing back down at the ring Steel had given me two weeks back. It hadn't been a traditional proposal. Our relationship was complicated. And that blue truck reminded me why I hadn't been able to say "yes" to Steel.

"Stop looking," Scarlet growled in frustration.

"Do you think he'll care . . . about the ring?" I only let Scarlet see how incredibly vulnerable Asher still made me feel.

"Oh, Dixie," she sighed and pulled me into a hug. "You know he won't. It's been three years. You've got to let Asher go for good."

I closed my eyes and let her hold me, because in that moment, I knew was right. She was always right. "How do I forget him, Scarlet?" The lilt in my voice made Scarlet squeeze a little tighter.

"Let yourself love Steel. He loves you. Be the girl he deserves," she replied. Scarlet then pulled back to look at me. Both her hands rested on my shoulders. "Asher Sutton broke you. He deserves for you to forget him. Steel Sutton, on the other hand, adores you. And he's nothing like his big brother. He gave you a ring, sweetie. It's time your heart let go of the wrong Sutton boy and fell in love with the one that deserves it."

I knew she was right. I just wasn't sure where to start. Not when everything still reminded me of the one who didn't love me back.

Four Years Ago . . .

I PATIENTLY SAT in daddy's truck while he filled the diesel tank with fuel. Jack's parking lot had begun to fill up. Jack's was a pool hall, that was also a bar, or maybe it was the other way around. A bar that was also a pool hall. I wasn't sure because I'd never been in there. If my daddy ever heard I was in there—and he would've found out quickly because Jack would've called him himself—he'd have thrown a fit.

The only reason I would want to go to Jack's anyway was because of the faded blue pickup truck that was currently parked outside the place. I'd seen three of the five Sutton boys climb from it and enter the establishment. The only one that mattered to me, however, had been the driver. Asher had sauntered inside like he owned the place. All smiles and too sexy for words in the jeans he'd been wearing.

He had those jeans on today at school. I had noticed them as well as the Malroy Bears Football tee-shirt he'd worn. Every day since the first day of school, Asher made sure to walk with me to at least a few of my classes. I knew he only did it to protect me and it worked. Emily James hadn't harassed me again, and because of that alone, high school was proving to be a lot easier than middle school had been for me.

The day I'd climbed into his truck in someone else's stinky, oversized gym clothes had changed me forever. I'd become more confident when dealing with Emily's cruel pranks and at some point, they simply stopped. The last day of middle school she had tripped me. I was walking down the hallway for the very last time with my arms full of my locker contents. When I fell, notebooks, pencils, and even a few tampons went flying into the air, landing all around me. But that had been it and, seemingly, her final act of cruelty toward me. Now it was October and, in a week, I'd be turning fifteen. Emily had never looked my way again since I'd began high school two months before.

Scarlet had texted me that she was going to Jack's tonight. She wanted me to go with her, lie to my parents, which was common for

Scarlet, but not for me. She knew before she even asked I wouldn't do it. But she asked me anyway like she always did. Now, sitting here and having watched Asher walk inside, made me wish I was braver, wilder, and didn't care so much about letting daddy down.

She'd tell me all about it tomorrow anyway. The girl Asher took to his truck. Who the twins Brent and Bray Sutton ended their heated night with. Who she, Scarlet, made out with in the dark. Or in front of everyone. To her, it didn't matter. Even though she had her eye on Steel Sutton these days. He was our age, and he was the Sutton boy to pursue for girls in our grade.

"You good with fried chicken? Jack's cooking up fried chicken. You can run in the back and get a bucket. Get some of them fries of his, too. We're fending for ourselves tonight."

Momma went to church on Wednesday nights. Her ladies' group bagged groceries and delivered them to the needy every week. Truth was she would have made us dinner if daddy had allowed her. But he insisted we would eat out so she wouldn't need to cook every night, and so we did. Every Wednesday night, just the two of us, and usually it was fried.

"That's fine with me," *I replied, a small thrill from possibly catching a glimpse of Asher again made my heart race. I didn't want to act overly excited about chicken from a bar, or Daddy would have gotten suspicious.*

"Let me use your phone," *he said, extending his hand to me.*

I didn't have anything to hide from him, so I gave him my phone without any hesitation.

Daddy took my phone and called Jack, telling him what we wanted. "While your momma is gone, we might as well live it up. Reckon you can whip us up some sweet tea?"

Lately, momma was on a health kick. It wouldn't last long because they never did, but she wanted daddy to consume less sugar and grease, which were the very things he enjoyed the most. She said he'd live longer that way. But he just ended up eating it whenever she wasn't around. Like tonight, for example.

"Yeah, I can." I might as well. If I said no, he'd just go get a beer from the case he hid inside the barn. The real kind, not the light version which momma bought for him.

Although the chance was slight I'd see Asher from the back where I'd enter and Jack would send a server, I still couldn't stop myself from getting giddy at the possibility. I had seen him today at school, and even though he'd talked to me and walked with me to three of my classes, always interested in what I was learning, my grades, and my new friends, I already couldn't wait to see him again. Because even when everyone around us was calling out his name, trying to get his attention, Asher only paid attention to me.

"Ask Jack to give us extra of that special sauce he makes," daddy added as I leapt from the truck. He must have been ravenous for extra sodium and a hearty dose of cholesterol.

"Okay," I replied, thinking to myself about all the mayonnaise and fat in that special sauce and how unhappy Momma would be about that. But I would do whatever he asked and make him happy. Besides, it would give me more time to stand there while the server ran to get the sauce, which gave me a better chance at catching a glimpse of Asher.

The large, heavy wooden door that had been painted red years before I was born was a familiar sight to me. I'd only entered Jack's through that back door. And only when daddy brought me here. I'd get the food, then pay and leave. I never got to go inside through the front entrance because Daddy didn't want me in a bar. High school students weren't served alcohol, but they were allowed inside. Everyone but me because Jack would rat me out.

Brandon Heely was standing just inside the door with a bag of food I knew was ours. "Hey, Brandon," I said politely. He'd been working here for years even though he should've been off at college by now. But he wasn't and probably never would be because he preferred to flip burgers at Jack's and riding his motorcycle around Malroy, pretending to be the badass he wanted to be, but never could be.

"Hey, Dix, here's your order."

"Thank you," I replied, reaching forward. "Daddy wants to add some extra special sauce," I added, praying he had to go to the front to get some from the cooler.

Brandon chuckled. "This is his third time ordering this week. Jack says your momma has him on a diet. Is that true? Because it ain't working if you ask me."

Third time! Jeez! Daddy! I hadn't realized he was sneaking off for greasy bar food that often.

"Yeah. She'll eventually give up or catch him."

Brandon sounded amused. "Stay right here. I'll go get the sauce."

This was my chance. "Okay."

As he turned to walk away, I slowly followed behind him. I crept closer to the swinging door and just when I thought I wasn't going to see anything before it closed in my face, I caught a glimpse of Asher, standing at the pool table, with a grin on his beautiful lips. His arm was propped on Andrea James, Emily's older, college age sister. She was leaning against him, enjoying herself and Asher doing the same. She worked here, had to be at least twenty, and like her sister Emily, she was gorgeous and curvy. Now I officially hated her.

Andrea was in heels, making her almost as tall as Asher. She was leaning in to whisper in his ear when the door closed and blocked my view of them. I slowly backed away. I'd seen enough. I knew Asher was popular with the older girls. He was popular with all the girls, regardless of their age. They all wanted him because he had it all—looks, charm and mystique. But I wanted him for other reasons altogether. Not that it mattered anyway. I was a kid to Asher, one he was following around to keep safe and protect from bullies at school. I was just a charity case to him and I knew that.

Brandon stepped back through the door with two containers of their famous sauce. "Here you go. Jack said to tell the old man he better not clog his arteries and have your momma up here giving him the what for."

I forced a smile. "I will. Thanks, Brandon. Have a good night," I said, before turning to rush out with our order. I was glad I hadn't gone with Scarlet. I'd seen enough through that door to last me for months. I didn't need to see anymore. My heart couldn't bear it.

I opened the door and sat the bag on the seat. Daddy pulled the order to the middle to peek inside, while I climbed back in the truck. "You get the extra sauce?"

"Yes, sir. But three times this week? Seriously? You need to admit that to Momma. Her healthy eating regimen is making you eat even worse. Greasy bar food isn't meant to be consumed more than once a week, Daddy. And even that's a lot for you. Enough to kill you."

Daddy sighed. "I'd much rather eat your momma's greasy food, but she's quit frying stuff."

"That's because she wants you to live a long time. Jack's cooking won't do that."

"I ain't gonna fuss with you about this. Your mother gives me enough grief. My granddaddy ate fried food and raw beef up until his ninety-sixth birthday, when he went on to be with the Lord. I'm just fine. Great genetics."

My great-granddad had lived a long life and I couldn't argue with that. I sighed and leaned my head back in my seat. I wanted to think about Asher, torture myself by going over all I'd seen at Jack's, but I knew I had to turn my thoughts to something else. Anyone else, just not a Sutton boy. Because they all reminded me of Asher. Even the youngest one who appeared part Native American. Their momma looked like that too. The rest were spitting images of their father. My daddy always said, "Vance Sutton reproduced and made twins of himself."

Vance Sutton must have been really handsome because he didn't have one ugly son. They were all striking. They just weren't all Asher. I really needed to stop thinking about him. .

"Tell me what you want for your birthday next week," Daddy asked, changing the subject.

I wanted Asher Sutton to notice that I had boobs and curves now and that I wasn't a little girl anymore. I wanted Asher Sutton to see me as something more than just a helpless kid who needed him to protect her from bad people. But these were all things that Daddy couldn't give me. No one could.

"Put whatever you were going to spend on me in my savings account for a car."

Daddy sighed. "How much you got saved? You've been working and saving for a couple years now and you still got one more year left. I'd think you had plenty by now. I told you I'd meet you half way. Whatever you save, I'll equal."

I wasn't sure what I wanted yet. To be safe, I was saving all I could. If I had extra money in the end, I could use it for any problems the car had later on. I didn't need anything else.

"I'm saving until I turn sixteen. Right now, the balance on my savings is five thousand even with interest."

Daddy released a whistle. "Lord, girl! I'm gonna have to take out a loan to meet you half way at that rate."

Of course, he was teasing. I replied, "guess you better start saving too."

That brought a deep belly laugh from him. I smiled and inhaled the greasy chicken smell filling the air. I might not have Asher Sutton, but I had a good life, and I was grateful for that.

chapter
TWO

Asher Sutton

MOMMA HADN'T MENTIONED the doctor wanted to put her on blood pressure medication. I remained calm while Frank Harrod told me how happy he was that she had agreed to take it. He'd gone on and on about how dangerous it was at her age not to treat high blood pressure. Why the fucking hell hadn't Doc John called me before now to let me know?

I pulled my truck into the gravel driveway outside the farmhouse I'd grown up in and I took a deep breath. I hadn't been here since Christmas. Even then, my visit had been a short one, I made sure of it. I'd wanted to run away. As far away from here as possible. The memories haunted the hell out of me whenever I got near this place.

A loud banging startled me and I jerked my head around to see Bray grinning at me like a fool. "You are home, motherfucker!" he said, gripping the frame of the door.

Bray was only twelve months younger than me and seeing him smile was rare. Brent, his twin, was the happy one. A grin was always on Brent's face while Bray normally scowled. Not much excited Bray, which only made me feel even guiltier for staying away so long, seeing him smiling at me like that.

I opened the door and grabbed the bag with the meds I had picked up and intended to force Momma to start taking right away. I couldn't lose her. There was a lot of fucked up in my life, but my momma was the one person I depended on to be there. I would like to think no one knew I was such a momma's boy, but the truth was, everyone knew. Then again, it wasn't just me. All four of my brothers loved our momma. She was our home. We knew as long as she was here in this house, we had a safe place to come back to.

"Don't look too excited to see me. I'll think you missed me," I teased Bray. He then grinned bigger, no longer trying to hide the fact he was pleased to see me home.

"Fuck that. I'm just glad you're here. 'Bout time you came back."

"Holy hell! That can't be my long-lost brother who thinks he's too good to come home." Brent called out from the front porch rail, before swinging his legs above it in one swift move we'd all perfected from our many years of jumping it. When his feet hit the ground, he took several long strides toward me before grabbing and hugging me bearlike.

As glad as Bray had been to see me, he hadn't been as excited as Brent. He slapped me on the back. "Momma's gonna be the happiest woman in Malroy," Brent said.

"No," Bray drawled. "The happiest woman in Malroy is Jenny Wilson. I spent a good thirty minutes with my head between her legs last night."

"Dude, fuck, you did not just say that," Brent replied, shaking his head.

I just chuckled. I missed this. Being away from my family and this place was so damn hard at times. Unable to help myself, I lifted my gaze to scan the yard, looking past it and toward the white picket fence that surrounded the house neighboring ours. I wondered if she was still living at home. If she looked older . . . Fuck, where did that come from? It only happened here, being so close to her. I normally didn't allow myself these thoughts because they were too dangerous, too destructive, and entirely pointless.

Brent said with his dimpled grin, "Momma's inside putting up some jam. She won't allow them strawberries to waste. She's been at it for two damn days. We'll have good ol' strawberry jam with our biscuits all year long."

"Reckon with you being home, we can coax her to use some of those berries to make us fried pies," Bray said. "Been craving one of them pies."

I wanted to talk to Momma alone. This shit with her not taking her medication was serious and I had to fix it. Then, I needed to leave. Run like hell, because at this moment, all I wanted to do was look back toward that white picket fence.

"Where are Steel and Dallas?" I asked Brent as he fell in step beside me walking toward the front porch of the house.

"Uh," he replied and glanced back at Bray before replying. I knew that look. Something was up. Fuck. I'd been gone too long. What other shit did I need to fix before I could leave again?

"Probably at the feed store," Brent added. "We were low on some stuff. Steel said he'd go get it. I'm sure Dallas rode with him. The white truck is gone. I don't see it." He was lying. His tone always gave him away.

"Motherfucker, you suck at that," Bray said, shaking his head and walking past us like it was a race. He took the steps two at a time, barging through the front door as if he were in a hurry to get away from everything behind him.

"What am I missing? 'Cause I'm definitely missing something,"

I asked, stopping on the steps, and turning from Brent's deer in the headlights expression to Bray's stiff back at my front.

"Just tell 'im," Bray said without looking back at us.

Brent didn't say a word. We all stood there for a moment. The silence was deafening, filling the air with growing tension. I shouted, "if something is wrong with one of them, I need to fucking know."

Bray dropped his hand from the door and turned to look at me. The hesitation I'd seen on Brent's face wasn't on his twin's. There was an annoyed glare instead. "They're fine. Everyone is just fucking fantastic. Calm your shit down," he replied, shifting his gaze from me to the yard at my rear as he sighed. I could see him trying to control his temper, another thing that set the twins apart. Brent didn't lose his very easily. Hell, you were lucky if you could piss him off. But Bray was a loaded gun. He'd blow the hell up fairly easily and I'd had to bail his ass out of trouble more times than I'd care to admit.

"Where are they?" I asked, looking at Bray.

Bray didn't look back at me. The muscle in his jaw ticked as he kept his gaze on the yard. He was thinking this through, whatever it was, and though I didn't like to be kept waiting, I also didn't want to come home and end up in a brawl in the yard before even giving my momma a hug.

"Steel has been dating Dixie for almost a year," Bray said. He spoke calmly, but the warning couldn't be missed. He was protecting our younger brother, without any idea whatsoever what he was protecting him from.

Everything around me started spinning. I grabbed the railing beside me, steadying myself, because this wasn't happening. I'd left to protect a secret, to protect Dixie . . . but this . . . holy fuck . . . what had I done?

This couldn't be fucking happening. I'd lost it all, walked

through hell for three long years, and I still walked through it daily. Every dream she appeared in reminded me that no one else would ever be enough. Lies had ruined my life. I wouldn't let them ruin hers too. And I sure as hell wouldn't let them ruin Steel's.

"Don't fuck this up for him. He worships you. Would do anything to please you. But he loves her," Bray warned me through his glare.

He didn't know what he was saying. None of them did. No one knew but me. I wasn't about to lose my shit because I was jealous. I'd learned to live with the jealousy that consumed me anytime I thought of someone touching her.

"Have they . . ." I couldn't even say it. My throat shut. I wanted to yell at the world, at how cruel it could be. The tightness in my chest and the rage pounding in my veins were emotions I knew all too well. Emotions I shouldn't be feeling. The mere idea of Dixie with someone else ripped me apart. I'd been living that nightmare for three fucking years, knowing I had no right to be jealous. I felt sick to my stomach that keeping my mouth shut had now led to this. But as horrified as I felt, all I could think about was Steel touching Dixie . . . my own fucking brother.

"Fuck!" I roared, stalking back through the yard, needing distance from everyone present. My heart was pounding so hard I thought it would leap from my chest. The range of emotions churning through me spread like a lightning bolt through my skull. "Motherfucking hell!" I yelled, throwing the bag of my momma's medication to the ground and grabbing my head with my hands. I felt dizzy, my eyes bugging from the pulse of the pain.

My knees went weak and I let them give way, squatting, resting my elbows on my thighs and holding my head through the pain. I'd run from Malroy to save us both. But while trying to save Dixie from what would haunt me for the rest of my life, I'd left my baby brother unprotected and free to walk into a horrible sin. Holy hell, how could I do this to him now? How could I let him turn into this same shell of a person I'd become?

"Asher?" Momma's voice rang out loud and clear from the porch. I let my hands fall as I looked up at her. She was standing tall with her apron on and her hands on her hips, staring at me. The pinched look on her face meant she was upset. The stained red spots all over her apron reminded me of happier times. Days when sneaking a strawberry without momma knowing was the only problem I had.

"You two had to go and tell him before he even got in the door? You little shits. I haven't seen my boy since Christmas and you upset him off the bat!" Momma scolded Bray and Brent before shaking her head and pointing at me. "Get up from there, for God's sake. You're too big to act like a five-year-old throwing a temper tantrum. Come see your momma and then tell me why the hell you went and got a prescription that I didn't ask for in the first place. I'll make you a fried pie while you explain." Her tone meant business and we knew that. "And you two," she added, waving the towel in her hand between the two of them. "Y'all should be ashamed. Ain't the way to do things!"

I stood, let the numbness wash over me. It was the only way I'd get through this. My own little brother would now pay for my mistake. The gaping hole in my chest grew bigger and bigger. Forcing myself to stop thinking about it for the moment, I picked up the bag of Momma's meds from the ground and moved toward the house, walking slowly onto the porch and into my momma's open arms. As her five-foot-seven frame held me tight, tears stung my eyes. I hadn't cried since the night I realized that I'd lost it all, or more accurately, the night I realized it had never been mine to have. Having Momma hold me made me want to break down like a little kid. But I held it together like the man they all expected me to be.

Four Years Ago . . .

I LIKED GIRLS. Better yet, I loved girls. I loved everything about them. The way they smelled, their soft skin, the curve of their bodies, the sound of their laughter. God put girls on this earth to make it a brighter place. I truly believed that.

The problem with that was that I loved all girls. I wasn't picky, couldn't choose just one when there were so many of them to choose from. When they touched my arm, whispered in my ear, promised with their mouths what their bodies would do, I didn't know how to turn them down.

Now and then, I got some loving from a girl who thought she'd change me for good. Make me just want her and her alone. But as soon as she realized I wasn't a one-woman man, all her sugar turned sour, the ugly came out, and I quickly moved on to another. I tried to avoid that kind of girl, but sometimes they snuck through my defenses.

Andrea James had a hint of sour lurking right under the surface. It was there. I sensed it immediately. She had curves in all the right places and she smelled like a wet dream, but I'd seen that gleam in her eyes before, and I wasn't willing to chance it. I made my excuses, blamed my momma, said that she needed me home. Not even Andrea James was brave enough to make my momma angry. After that, I headed out the door. Jack's place was all we had in town. For a good time, that's where we went. I looked forward to college when a pool hall bar wasn't the only thing to entertain me.

"You sure your momma wouldn't let you stay out a little longer?" Andrea called from the steps in front of Jack's as I was climbing into my truck.

I wanted to answer back, "I'm sure she would, but you've got that crazy in your eyes I ain't willing to tangle with." Being a nice guy and all, I replied, "yeah, I'm sure. Promised I'd help her hang some shelves." Now that was a lie, but sometimes a lie was needed to save yourself from imminent disaster.

Shame Andrea James was the crazy sort. Guess I should have figured *that out before I let her rub up on me. Her younger sister was a real mean bitch. That I knew for a fact. Once I was told she had been the one harassing Dixie, I made sure that didn't happen anymore. Dixie was the sweetest kind of girl there was. The kind you looked at, wanted to get closer to, but knew you shouldn't. She was not the kind of girl you took to your truck. She'd never be that girl.*

I knew I spent too much time watching Dixie. I liked to be near her as much as I could. Dixie smelled sweeter, laughed brighter, talked softer, and her eyes saw deeper than any other girl I knew. It was hard to ignore Dixie Monroe. And if I was younger, I wasn't sure I'd be able to keep her at an arm's length. But I wasn't younger, I was three years older than her, and had no business looking her way. Instead, I let myself enjoy little innocent tastes of her. Small moments spent in Dixie's company. That was enough for me. And like always, just before I turned down the dirt road, the one that led to my house, I glanced over toward Dixie's home. This was one of my little tastes of her. Because sometimes I saw nothing, but sometimes I saw glimpses of her life, glimpses of her, and I couldn't look away.

Tonight, I was lucky. The full moon and the front porch light illuminated her house and yard. And Dixie sat there on the bottom step of her porch, her feet bare and her knees tucked beneath her chin, her head turning in my direction as I drove past her. Although it was too far to see the reaction on her face, I knew she recognized my truck. And she didn't look away.

Bray swore Dixie had a crush on me. He'd been saying that for years. I didn't know why as Steel was her age and he was popular in their grade. I knew that if she showed any interest in him, he'd jump at the opportunity to make her his.

Something made me stop the truck in the middle of the road, put it in park, and look back at Dixie Monroe. I knew that pulling into her drive and walking to her wasn't a good idea. I wanted to join her, to hear her laugh and watch her smile, to simply be near her for a little while, but I knew better.

Instead, I chose to sit here in my truck. Let my presence communicate all I couldn't say. That I saw her. That I wished things were different. But for both our sakes, it was best that I stayed in my truck. I was too old for her. And nothing could change that.

I figured one day, once we were both adults, the three years between us wouldn't matter anymore. But would she be in love by then? Maybe planning on marrying someone from around here. Or would she go off to college and meet a guy there? Would we ever get a chance? I didn't like thinking I'd never get one.

Dixie's gaze was locked on my truck. I remained parked on that dirt road, opening my door and stepping out of the truck to lean against it. With nothing between us but darkness and only moonlight making me visible to her, I crossed my arms over my chest, and just watched her back.

For once, I let my thoughts drift to all the "what ifs" I never allowed my mind to entertain. I wondered what Dixie was thinking in that moment. She didn't move and she didn't look away. Many girls had tried to change me, but I knew that only Dixie was the girl I'd change for. The only girl I'd ever need.

When she stood, her sudden movement jerked me from my thoughts. Our watching game was over. I'd wanted her to stay there longer. Make this moment between us last for as long as it could. But I knew it shouldn't, as innocent as it had been.

For a second, I thought she was going to walk to me. Part of me wished she would, although I had no idea what I would say if she did. Words weren't necessary during this perfect moment between us. But she didn't come to me. She just raised her hand, gave me a little wave, and walked inside her house without looking back at me. I waited until her bedroom light came on, and only then got back in my truck and drove off. Something happened between us that night, something shifted, and even though no words were exchanged, we both knew things would never be the same.

chapter
THREE

Dixie Monroe

I STOOD ON the porch looking out. I could only see the roof of the Sutton house as it was on the other side of the hill. But I knew it was there because I often stood here and let my gaze settle on that tin roof. Memories still haunted me, breaking my heart over and over again as I let myself remember.

When I'd bumped into Steel last August outside the grocery store, I dropped my bag and the contents rolled free, causing both of us to scramble to catch them. When Steel grabbed a can of soup and handed it to me, the smile on his face was so similar to Asher's that it caught me by surprise and took my breath away.

Steel had been in my grade during school. He was the Sutton boy I should've been drawn to, but he hadn't been. Asher was all I could see. From the time I turned thirteen and he had given me a ride home from school in his wonderful old pickup truck, I'd been completely consumed by him.

He didn't feel the same way, of course. I was too young for

him then. But we'd still grown up running through the same fields and swimming in the same swift creek. He was my friend, even though he was older and the most popular boy in town.

That entire year I'd worshipped him from afar. When he asked if I needed a ride, I always said yes. Then that summer before the ninth grade, my body had decided to change.

My first day of high school, Asher became my shadow. If any guy even looked my way, his mere presence had them scurrying the other way. I loved it. Although I hadn't understood why he was doing it.

It wasn't until October of the year I turned fifteen that he made a move. Asher Sutton backed me up against his truck and placed his hands on both sides of my body. I knew it was all about to change. When his lips touched mine, my body lit like a firecracker, and we were inseparable after that. He took a football scholarship at the local junior college instead of going to a larger school just so he could be near me. He said he'd wait and that he could always transfer to somewhere else when I graduated.

But that didn't happen. None of that happened.

One night he was loving me, telling me he wanted me forever. The next day he couldn't even look me in the eyes. And he never told me why.

The crunch of gravel under the tires snapped me out of my trance. I'd let myself be carried away by the memories, as I always tended to do. I squinted against the glare of the sun. Steel's white truck was coming down the drive. He was here to tell me Asher was home. I wasn't sure what he wanted to do. When Asher came home for Christmas, I was in Oklahoma at my grandmother's. I didn't have to face him then. But now, if Asher was home, I'd have to face him with Steel. I wasn't ready for that, and I doubted I would ever be ready.

The truck stopped and I watched as Steel jumped down

from his jacked-up raised vehicle. He looked good in his worn jeans, but no one compared in my eyes to his older brother. And I hated myself for it. Steel didn't deserve this. Not when he had been so good to me.

"Hey," I said, forcing a smile I didn't feel as Steel walked up the steps. His serious expression was fixed on me and it made me fearful of what he had come to say.

He ducked his head a moment and sighed, before looking back at me. "You already know, don't ya?" But he already knew the answer from the look on my face.

I nodded.

Steel released another deep sigh and stuck his hands in his pockets. "I ain't seen him yet. Bray called to warn me he was here. Asher knows about us. Bray told him, Dixie."

He knew about us? I had a million questions to ask at that moment: why Bray had told him, what he had said exactly, how Asher had reacted, whether he was upset. But I didn't ask any of them.

"Okay," was all I could say without betraying all I was feeling.

Steel took one more step toward me, standing now only a few inches from me. His light blue eyes were the same as Asher's, but the golden hue of his hair was fittingly different, matching his boyish optimism, even though he wasn't looking all that optimistic at that very moment. "Both of us are gonna have to face him. Bray don't think he's leaving soon and I don't want him to. I miss him, you know. I want him around. I know Momma wants him around too. And I think he needs us, Dixie. So, this thing between you and me," he said, with a grin tugging on his lips, "is something he'll have to deal with. I think he's gonna be okay. We just need to get it over with. You both need some closure."

Closure. For the past three years, Scarlet had been saying the same thing to me. But I didn't even know what closure was. If

Asher suddenly told me why he stopped loving me, would that actually make it better? Would I then be able to move on? Or would it make it even worse? That wound might never heal, but at least now I knew how to pretend.

"Come on, baby," he said, reaching out to take my hand and tug me gently to him. "He's my big brother, I want this to be okay with us . . . and also him. Because I love the both of you."

"You go spend time with your brother. We will deal with bringing me into things after you've caught up. I don't want to cause anyone to be uncomfortable," I replied, hoping to buy myself more time to prepare for the inevitable.

Steel pressed a kiss to the top of my head. "He'll be okay with this. Once he sees how we feel, it'll all be good, I promise."

I knew that Steel completely believed this. And I let him. Maybe he was right? Really, what did I know? It wasn't that Asher verbally ever said that he hated me. He just never acknowledged me again. When I went to his house, after calling several times and him never answering the phone, he'd looked right through me, and then he left town. He went to stay at his uncle's in Texas for a month and no one had an explanation to give me. They all looked at me with pity in their eyes.

When Asher returned, it was as if the man didn't know who I was. The Asher who had loved me so fiercely was gone and in his place stood an emotionless, cold stranger. He then accepted a scholarship to the University of Florida and I never saw him again.

I was left to claw my way out of despair all on my own, never knowing what I had done to lose him. Then just when I thought I had my heartbreak finally under control, Asher came back.

Four Years Ago . . .

I WAS NOW fifteen years old and I had one more year until I got my car.

My body had finally started developing, giving me curves where I never had them, and even boobs I was no longer ashamed of when I looked at myself in the mirror.

I knew all this wasn't enough to get Asher Sutton's attention, not in the way I so desperately wanted it. But it made me feel less like a child in front of him, less like a little girl he was protecting from bullies at school. That year, Steel Sutton had also begun talking to me in class, even more so since my body had started changing, and even though my infatuation with his brother was still consuming my every thought, I knew that at some point, I had to let myself date somebody else.

Steel was probably not going to be that "somebody" because I'd not only have to be around Asher, but hiding my feelings for Asher while dating Steel would be hard. Impossible even. I needed someone else to date, but he would have to be a brave soul. Asher was around me more and more lately and since our little staring game in the dark, he was talking to me even more. I rarely walked to a class that Asher didn't walk me to these days. He was slowly becoming a permanent fixture around me. Our strange night was never mentioned. I'd sat there on the step wondering if he wanted me to walk to him. If he was waiting on me. Finally, I'd decided he'd have to come to me. He hadn't, of course. He was Asher Sutton. And I was just an inexperienced young girl with no idea how to handle him, or how he wanted me to react.

Today though, I was older, and I finally looked my age. I had plenty to be happy about and I had decided that I didn't need Asher to be happy. I was turning over a new leaf.

"Dixie, you have . . . uh, company," my mother called up the stairs. We were about to leave for school. Who was here and why? Was this another birthday surprise? I'd awakened to my favorite breakfast, chocolate cake on a plate, a tradition they began when I was four. I'd wanted my birthday cake so bad, I'd asked God in my prayers for my parents to let me have cake for breakfast on my birthday. They'd found that funny and not wanting me to think God wasn't listening to me, they'd given

me cake for breakfast.

That wasn't a surprise, of course, but during breakfast they had also given me a camera, though I'd only asked my dad to make a deposit in my car fund and nothing more. He'd done that, and then he bought the camera too, because he knew it was something I was into lately. Last summer, I'd found an old camera in the attic and ever since then, I'd been taking photos, mostly of people, the kind of action shots I'd seen in magazines.

His voice stopped me as I hit the first step. Asher Sutton was in my house, talking to my parents, on my birthday. I glanced down at the skirt and top I was wearing. Secretly, I'd thought of Asher when I picked them out, hoping he'd see me in them and like the way I looked.

"Yes sir, I'm thinking of the University of Florida . . ."

"Good choice, although Alabama's my favorite, I'll give them Gators a cheer, when they aren't playing Bama, of course." Daddy's reply was predictable, I thought. They were talking football. Asher was thinking of going all the way to Florida? That was so far. I'd have three full years left of high school while he was away at Florida, falling in love, maybe getting engaged, which immediately made my stomach feel sick.

I slowly walked the rest of the way down the stairs and put a smile on my face. Asher was in my house and he was here to see me, not to bring Momma something his mother had made for her, or to borrow a tool from Daddy. Asher was here for me.

"Hey," I said, as I entered the living room.

Asher turned, a sexy smile appearing on his face with ease. "Happy birthday, Dixie," he replied.

"Thank you," I replied, beaming.

"I figured I'd give you a ride to school on such an important day. Was driving by and thought it would be nice to visit the birthday girl." He paused and looked back at my parents. "That is, if it's okay with the both of you?"

My mother's eyes got that knowing light in them. I knew she was reading the wrong thing into this, but I couldn't correct her in front of Asher.

"Reckon it is, if I can have your word that you'll treat my girl like the lady she is. I've heard about that truck of yours. Dixie ain't one of them girls."

I blushed from embarrassment, wanting to crawl under the coffee table and hide there forever.

"Yes, sir. You have nothing to worry about. Dixie's my friend, and I respect her. I like spending time with her, as a friend, only as a friend."

Asher had just said I was his friend three times and that was all the wake up call I needed to stop me from getting silly ideas about him being here, picking me up for school on my birthday. He only saw me as his friend and that was all.

Daddy didn't look very convinced. But he nodded, indicating he was buying it. "Known you since you were born. You're a good boy, even if you've got a bit of a reputation with girls. I trust you'll do right by my Dixie."

Oh, good Lord, this was getting more embarrassing by the second. I hurried to the door saying, "we need to go or we'll be late," and opening it quickly. The cool morning breeze helped my heated cheeks, but it would take an ice storm to cool them.

"Have a good day, honey. Wear your seatbelt," Momma called.

I nodded, and kept hurrying to his waiting truck. I feared that if we didn't get away soon, dad would be asking Asher about his intentions and whatnot.

I climbed in the passenger side of the truck and it dawned on me then that the other Suttons weren't here. Asher shared this truck with the twins and they rode to school together every day.

Asher got inside with a chuckle. "Don't worry about them, Dix. They're just parents being parents. No need to be embarrassed."

"Where are your brothers?" I asked, wanting to forget that scene inside. I wasn't looking at him, I couldn't do that yet.

"*They got another ride.*"

"*Why?*"

"*Because I didn't want them in here to see me give you this.*" I looked up from my lap to see a small silver box with a shiny pink bow on top. Asher was giving me a present. A boy had never given me a gift, not on my birthday at least, unless you count the white bunny Davey Miller gave me way back in first grade. It was the same bunny he napped with his entire kindergarten year which made me feel pretty special at the time.

I reached for it. My hand trembled a little and I hoped he didn't notice. I was excited, part of me wishing he'd left it on my doorstep so that I could open it privately. I knew that even if it were a rock, I would love it. It didn't matter to me what was inside that box. It was from Asher and that made it precious.

"*You gonna hold it like it might bite you or go ahead and open it?*" he teased.

"*The wrapping is so pretty I hate to mess it up,*" I replied, no longer able to contain the big smile tugging at my lips.

"*Thanks. I did it myself.*"

I wasn't sure I believed that. "*Sure you did.*"

His eyebrows immediately shot up. "*Hell yeah I did, ask my momma. She supplied the wrapping paper and the bow. But I wrapped it. Honestly, I did.*"

Now I didn't want to ruin the wrapping even more. I'd keep it like this forever.

"*Open it, Dix,*" he said, smiling.

Fine. But I wasn't going to tear the paper. I unwrapped it as gently as I could. Sliding out the small box, I realized I was holding my breath. I quickly inhaled before I passed out in front of him and embarrassed myself even more.

I lifted the top from the box and my heart swelled even more from seeing what it held inside. It wasn't because of the price of the gift or its beauty. It was because he'd remembered something about me that not *many people knew.*

"How did you remember this?" I held The Little Mermaid sterling silver charm that would now complete my Princess bracelet. They discontinued it when I was nine years old, before I could complete my collection. I'd cried that day when Momma told me she couldn't find one anywhere. Asher had been borrowing a saw from Daddy and he'd seen me in tears. When I told him why I was crying, he had hugged me, assured me that one day this wouldn't be a big deal to me. I cried that it would always be a big deal because The Little Mermaid had been my favorite. I'd wanted that charm from the moment I got my bracelet, but it was always sold out everywhere we looked.

I'd forgotten all about that, but he clearly hadn't. That bracelet was still in my jewelry box, missing its last charm. Until now.

Tears stung my eyes and I smiled as I held it in my hand like the priceless treasure it was to me.

"When a beautiful girl cries, a boy never forgets why," Asher replied softly.

chapter
FOUR

Asher Sutton

DALLAS HAD LET his black hair grow long and it was now pulled back in a ponytail. When I came home for Christmas, he'd been tucking it behind his ears, but it hadn't been pulled back yet. He had our mother's green eyes and my grandmother's Native American skin tone, also like mom. She always said Dallas was the prettiest of us all and we gave him hell about it. He was also fucking spoiled, being Momma's favorite, her baby.

I took a big drink from the milk Momma fixed me and noticed my baby brother's grin. Dallas was clearly looking forward to Steel getting back because he thought we would fight. And Dallas loved a good fight and placed bets on underground fights all the time, thinking I didn't know it.

"You want another pie?" Momma asked, glancing over her shoulder as she dropped another pastry into the frying pan.

"No, thanks, I'm good," I replied.

"I want one, Momma. Fighting makes me hungry," Dallas

drawled, Brent shoving him and causing Dallas to lean off, before he cackled with laughter.

"Ain't no fighting going on around here. And you two stop rough-housing in my kitchen." Momma spoke, frowning at them both.

"Can I still have another pie?" Dallas asked, seriously pouting. He was seventeen years old and pouting over a fucking fried pie.

"Of course. Go sit and be good," she replied, Dallas winking at her, and causing her to roll her eyes before going back to frying the pies.

"You're a dipshit, you know that, don't you?" I said, as he pulled out a chair, turned it around and straddled it.

"Missed you, too," he replied, trying his charm on me, like he did on the rest of the world. He could be a smartass one minute and a charmer the next.

"Your pretty face don't work on me," I said, taking another drink of my milk.

"He's here," Bray announced as he walked into the kitchen. "Just saw him drive up. You gonna play nice?" He was looking directly at me.

I wasn't mad at Steel. I was angry because this shit was going to hurt him, too. He'd be changed forever, the same as I had been, and all I ever wanted was to keep them safe. But I'd failed. My leaving hadn't helped anything. It had simply made it worse.

"I'm good," I replied when I realized all four sets of eyes were on me.

The screen door opened again and this time it was Steel who walked in. He looked straight at me and stopped. He looked nervous.

"About time you finally got home," I said casually, rising from my chair.

He took a step back, then froze, taking a deep breath. I'd

eased him with my words.

"I haven't seen you since Christmas," I said, closing the space between us and pulling him into a hug. "Missed you, bro."

The tension in his shoulders slowly relaxed as Steel hugged me back. "Glad you're home," he finally replied, and it sounded like he meant it.

"Awww, shi—crap," Dallas whined, catching himself before he cursed in front of Momma. "I was hoping for some action. You two are gonna be all mushy and sh—stuff."

"Stop being a douche," Bray growled at Dallas.

Momma spun and pointed her spoon at Bray. "You say douche in my kitchen again and I'll send you to the store to buy some. You hear me?"

Momma didn't seem to care we were all men now. She still treated us like we were little boys. Bray nodded and mumbled an apology. Once, he'd called Brent a pussy in front of her. Momma took him to the grocery store and made him buy tampons. When they got to the checkout, she made Bray hand the tampons directly to the cashier and then take the sack once the lady bagged them. For a thirteen-year-old boy, that had been traumatic. Bray never called anyone a pussy in front of Momma again. In fact, he hadn't used that word again until he finally got some actual pussy a few years after that.

"Since we're all here together and everyone is good, why don't we leave Momma to her television shows and homemade wine, and take this party down to Jack's. It's Karly Walsh's birthday and everyone's headed there tonight." Brent spoke, his eyes meeting mine. He still didn't trust us to sit around with Momma present in case I decided to say something to Steel.

"Sounds good! I'd forgotten about Karly's party," Dallas said, jumping up, his fried pie all forgotten.

"Watch him," Momma replied. "He ain't old enough to be

going to one of them parties or Jack's." Momma pointedly looked at me. The twins and myself had been going to Jack's well before we were seventeen. She always expected me to keep them safe and out of harm's way. And even with me being gone, she still relied on me to look after them whenever I came back home.

"I'll keep him out of jail," I promised as we all headed for the door.

"Take this fried pie," momma called out to Dallas. He turned around and took the fried strawberry pie she'd wrapped in a napkin for him. Dallas kissed her cheek and she grinned, looking up at her six-foot-three baby and patting his face like an infant.

Some things never changed. Except that my baby brother was now as tall as me.

Four Years Ago . . .

DEEP DOWN, I never expected this. I knew that my walking Dixie to classes would keep most guys back. But I should've been prepared for guys like Sellers Brachen to be cocky enough to walk up to Dixie right in front of me.

"Heard it's your birthday," Sellers drawled as I stood there and watched Dixie blush and stammer over her words. Sellers came from money. His dad was the head of the boosters and we had top of the line equipment on the field and in the locker room thanks to his contributions. Sellers was a good running back. And now he was pissing me off.

"Yes," she managed to respond. He clearly made her nervous and I wasn't sure I liked that much.

"Well, happy birthday, Dixie." He then turned his attention to me for a second and I could see the challenge in his eyes. Dumbass. I wasn't going to compete with him. Dixie wasn't a prize to be won.

"What are you doing after school?"

She stammered again, then replied. "Nothing. Going home."

He gave her a crooked grin, stepping closer to her. "That's a shame. On your birthday, you should go have some fun. How about going to get a cupcake? Then I'll take you out to see my new colt that was just born last week."

I was sure she was going to turn him down until he mentioned the new colt. Dixie loved horses.

"Oh, really? Okay, yes, I'd like to see the colt." She was less awkward now, smiling brightly at him. Sellers' smile changed too because Dixie's smile did that to a guy.

"We've got practice," I reminded Sellers.

"Only till four. Dixie, can you wait until four for me?"

She briefly glanced at me. I had no time to react. What was she expecting me to say? Did she want me to stop her?

"Sure. I'll, uh, do my homework, then come out to the parking lot."

Shit. Not what I wanted to hear.

"I'll be looking for you. Highlight of my week," he told her with a wink. He fucking winked. Like a douchebag.

Once he was gone, I tried to collect my thoughts, decide what I was going to say. I didn't know how to warn her away. He wasn't good enough for her.

"This is my class. Thanks for walking me. I'll see you later," Dixie said. She broke into my thoughts with her voice and then was gone before I could say anything.

Shit.

Fuck.

I wasn't okay with this.

But what could I do to stop it? She was a freshman. Sellers was a junior. Not a big deal to most people. He hadn't done anything I hadn't done. My reputation was probably worse than his. I was the one she needed to be protected from.

Goddammit. I just fucked up.

"You look like you're about to go jump off a ledge," Bray said,

snapping me back from my thoughts.

"Not today," I replied. *Although pushing Sellers off a ledge didn't seem like a bad idea.*

"Dixie," *was all Bray said. Just her name. Like it was all the explanation needed for my current demeanor.*

"What?" *I was annoyed that the little fucker saw too much. He paid too close attention.*

"Don't act stupid. You're the smartest one out of the five of us."

Actually, Bray was the smartest. His grades just didn't reflect it. He had an explosive temper that was hard to control. Since he was a little boy, we'd had to deal with it. "Bray, I'm not in the mood for games. What do you mean by that?"

Bray sighed as if my question exhausted him. "She's fifteen today, older, but not old enough to make it alright for you. That's what I fucking mean."

Out of all my brothers, Bray was the one who didn't let anything get past him. He was the one who saw it all, soaked everything in. And in moments like these, that insight might get him thrown from a window.

"Dixie is my friend. Just like she's your friend."

Bray laughed. "Oh, no. I'm not whacking my dick while fantasizing of fucking her."

"Jesus! What the hell is wrong with you?" *I growled, knowing all too well that I couldn't deny it.*

"Lighten up. She's grown up overnight. I'm not blaming you. Just saying you need to admit it and do something about it before someone else does. Because, believe me, brother, they will."

"What are y'all talking about?" *Brent interrupted. The twin I liked. The one who wasn't a nosey ass fucker.*

"Asher's wanting Dixie. Time he did something about it. Admitted that shit."

"Oh, yeah, you really should. Sellers is already talking about her. Move fast, bro, or perish."

Not what I wanted to hear.

"I've got literature, I think. Fuck, I don't know for certain. Either way, I gotta go. Do something, Asher. Get on it."

Those were Bray's parting words as he turned and jogged toward the gym. There weren't any classes that way. His lit class was in the opposite direction.

"Reckon he's going to meet someone?" Brent asked as we both watched him jog away.

"I wouldn't be surprised."

"How does he keep his grades up?"

That was easy. *"He's brilliant. Crazy as shit and a fucking genius."*

Brent nodded. *"Yeah, I guess you're right."*

There was no guessing to it. I knew I was right. My brother was a force to be reckoned with.

"Can I ask you something, Asher?"

I turned to Brent. *"Yeah."*

He glanced at Bray's retreating form, then looked back at me. *"Do you think he's okay? Like, mentally stable?"*

"Yeah. Why?"

"Because . . . sometimes he gets this darkness in his eyes. Like he's not there. Like he goes somewhere else in his mind. Somewhere I never want to be."

I knew the answer to that, but it wasn't my secret to tell. Instead, I replied, *"he's fine. Just Bray being Bray."* Because that much was obviously true.

chapter
FIVE

Dixie Monroe

AS WE WALKED into Jack's, Steel's hand tightened around mine. He'd texted me to meet him here. The only place in town to do anything, even though they didn't serve alcohol to minors, or at least that's what they told everyone. I'd seen a waitress bring a Sutton boy a beer more than once in the past three years I'd been allowed to actually come inside the front door. When I drove up and saw Asher's truck, I called Steel and he came outside to meet me. He assured me Asher was fine with us being together and that he'd been all smiles.

Was it wrong of me to feel disappointed that Asher was happy I was with his brother? Shouldn't I want him to be okay with this? Steel loved me. Steel wanted to marry me. Steel wouldn't toss me out like yesterday's trash.

But . . . now Asher was home.

I scanned the crowd. I could lie and tell myself I wasn't looking for Asher, but I was. I craved to see him and I had to get a handle on this. I was happy he was fine with me dating Steel, and it bothered me, too.

Brent's laughter caught my attention and I knew Scarlet was probably with him. But my eyes didn't seek Brent or Scarlet. They sought Asher who was sitting on a bar stool, holding a cue, watching Brent taunt Bray. The smile on Asher's face wasn't the heart-stopping one I'd once loved so much. Instead, it was a sad one. Did coming home make him sad? Once, I would've been able to wrap my arms around him and ask him what was bothering him. He would've told me and we could've worked right through it together.

"Want a Coke?" Steel asked as he pulled me in his brother's direction.

I wasn't sure what I wanted.

I shook my head and Steel bent his to kiss the top of mine. "I swear, babe, it's okay," he whispered in my ear.

He thought I was worried about Asher being upset about us. But what really worried me was how I would react to being near Asher again, after all this time. Would I be able to breathe? Would my heart hurt too much?

I looked for Scarlet, but I only saw Brent. He looked up from the pool table where he was watching Bray sink a ball, his smile wavering. He wasn't sure about this. Great. Had Steel been wrong? "Guess we're all together again. About damn time. Scarlet's on her way," Brent said with a genuine smile, before he winked at me and collected his stick, then walked over to the table.

Bray straightened and glanced back at me. His frown told me he wasn't on board. That this was a bad idea. I couldn't help but agree with Bray. But this was something Steel wanted for us.

"Hey, Em, why don't you come entertain Asher while I take his place in this game," Bray called to Emily James. Damn him. Was he doing this on purpose? I'd watched Emily paw all over Asher after he dumped me. I hated it then and it still made my skin crawl just thinking about it.

"What the hell ever," Steel said grinning. "If Asher is out, then I'm in. You had your turn. I'm up." Steel left me to walk over to the pool table.

I refused to glance over at Asher and Emily freakin' James. I knew she was tall with long legs. She had big fake boobs her momma bought her when she was eighteen years old. I also knew she'd spread her legs for Asher more than once. Word had gotten around. It didn't hurt any less now than it did back then. Emily of all people. Asher knew how she'd once treated me. And he'd done it anyway.

"He's not paying Em any mind. Stop tensing up or Steel's gonna notice," Dallas whispered in my ear. The youngest Sutton boy was the largest and the most perceptive by far. He studied crowds and body language like it was his chosen profession. "Ash ain't into fake titties anyway," he added, smirking all amused.

I glanced up at him and he shrugged as if to say, "what? You know I'm right."

"Nothing's fake about her legs," I replied in a bitter tone that I hated myself for. Dallas's gaze flicked over my shoulder in the direction of Emily's lone voice. It came from where Asher was seated. "Yeah, true," Dallas replied, "but once a pair of legs have been wrapped around the hips of every male in the county, what's between them ain't the glory land that it was before all the wrappings."

I couldn't stop the laugh that burst forth. Dallas's eyes met mine and he grinned, obviously pleased with himself for his comment. "That's more like it," he said. "Don't none of us want to see you all frowning. We love Ash and we're thrilled he's home, but we want the whole group to be alright again. To lay all the bullshit to the side."

In other words, I had to get over Asher.

I nodded and immediately replied. "Yes, we do." Because there was nothing I wanted more in the world than not to feel the pain slicing through me every time I thought of Asher. For three long years, I'd been heartbroken. When would it end? Would it ever?

"Come here, baby," Steel said, drawing my attention over to him. He was holding out his pool stick. "Show this smartass how it's done. I'm sick of watching Bray beat the shit outta everyone at this table."

Steel. I was here with Steel. He loved me. That was a truth I could count on.

I walked to him, his hand sliding around my waist, pulling me close. We were always like this, but having Asher a few feet away from us, made it feel like I was on a stage, being watched, judged and accused. I hated that feeling.

"I'm gonna head out. I'll see y'all at the house," Asher said, standing up, before walking away without another word. The silence that fell as he left made it all even more awkward. He hadn't wanted me here. He never wanted me around.

"Guess I was pushing it. My bad. I shoulda eased him into this." Steel spoke, looking over at Bray. When Asher wasn't around, it was Bray that the rest of the Sutton boys looked to, him being the second oldest, even if by only five minutes.

"Yeah, dipshit," Brent said. "Probably shoulda not called her baby." He then slapped the back of Steel's head and reached for his drink on the table. "He was just starting to relax."

Steel groaned and ran his hand through his hair: "I'll talk to him. Damn, this is fucked up. He shouldn't care anymore."

I didn't want to be standing here listening to this conversation. I was the problem and I felt even more out of place and in the way than ever before. "Maybe I should go home," I finally said, speaking up and reminding Steel that I was here, listening to it all.

He looked up at me and grimaced. "Sorry about this, but

yeah, I need to go and talk to Ash. I don't want him running off again. Momma would be heartbroken if he didn't stick around for a while. And we all miss him."

I nodded. I understood. I just wished it wasn't this way. But then again, I'd been wishing for a lot of things for as long as I'd known Asher Sutton. Repeated wishes wear you thin. Especially when they don't come true.

Four Years Ago . . .

I SAID YES to Sellers for one reason. And that reason wasn't fair. Sellers was being nice, he was just flirting, but my using him to show Asher I was more than a little girl to protect had been wrong. Yet, I said yes knowing it was wrong. Now I needed to tell him no. Maybe even tell him the truth, as embarrassing as the truth was to admit.

Asher hadn't walked me to my last two classes. My plan hadn't worked. Instead, it backfired in my face. Maybe now he thought I had Sellers to protect me, not that I needed protecting. Frustrated with the whole situation, I planned exactly what I would say to Sellers after his practice was finished. I even wrote it all down, read over it a few times, made sure I was completely prepared.

Five minutes before packing up my things and heading down to the field house, the door to the library opened and a very sweaty Asher walked in. I was the only one in the library. Even the librarian had left for the day. She'd said I could stay and do my homework until after practice ended. Either Asher was here to see me or he had a book he wanted to check out so badly, he'd left practice early to do it.

He stood inside the room, his large frame releasing an enormous amount of energy. My heart started beating faster, but then again, it always did around Asher. His gaze scanned the library, locked on me, before he approached with long, aggressive strides, and a determined look on his face.

"What are you doing?" I asked, standing up and getting ready to leave.

"Don't go out with Sellers," was all he said. I wanted that to mean more than it did. I wanted it to mean he didn't want me with Sellers because . . . well, he wanted me with him. But I knew that was a fantasy I couldn't allow myself to entertain.

"Do you not like Sellers?"

He shook his head no, but replied "I like Sellers just fine. I just don't like Sellers with you."

Asher's words were giving food to my fantasy world and I knew reality would soon slap me in the face again.

"Why?"

He stood there staring at me for what seemed like an eternity, but probably no longer than a few moments. "Just meet me out at my truck. Is that okay with you? I need to shower and get my things first."

I could have been strong here and said I was going with Sellers, even though I hadn't been planning on doing that. Asher didn't know that.

"I need to tell Sellers," I said, instead.

His shoulders seemed to ease some, but not completely. He stood at a distance from me, his body wound, tense and alert. He just replied, "I'll tell him."

I wasn't okay with that. "I should tell him," I said.

Asher sighed. "Fine. You tell him. But do it now."

Then he turned and headed for the door. There was no other explanation. Nothing. Not a word.

"Asher," I called, needing something more from him. Any answer.

"Yeah?" he asked, looking back at me, but holding the door with one hand.

"Why?" That was all I could manage to say without showing him all I was feeling.

"I," he paused, looking torn over what to say exactly. "Just . . . please . . . Dix."

Somehow, that was all I needed to hear at that moment. I didn't need anything more.

"Okay," I whispered.

He smiled at me with relief in his eyes, then opened the door and left. Alone in the library again, the smell of books returned to my senses and the silence became almost deafening. But now those things would forever hold a memory for me. One I'd never forget. It may not mean much, but I couldn't stop a small smile.

I slipped my books back into my bag, placing Sellers' speech in my pocket. I wouldn't be needing it. I was going to be honest with him and tell him the truth, one that had suddenly changed in the last few minutes.

There was a parking lot between the school and the field house. I spotted Sellers walking my way. He was already showered and dressed, in a pair of jeans and a football tee shirt, his hair still damp, but styled in that messy way he always wore. I knew that being honest with him was the best thing to do, but I still felt bad about it.

"You ready?" he asked while grinning.

"Uh, about that, thank you for the invite. It was very nice and any other time I would have enjoyed going. But Asher . . . he's . . . ah . . . asked me to go with him. I've wanted that for a very long time. It wouldn't be right to go with you when my mind would be stuck on Asher."

I felt like I stumbled on my explanation. Did it even make sense to anyone but me?

Sellers gave me a crooked grin. "So that's where he went so quickly after practice."

"Again, thank you, and I'm so sorry."

"It's okay, Dixie. I get it."

"Thanks," I repeated, quickly turning and walking away, eager to leave this awkward conversation. I hurried toward Asher's truck.

"You're welcome," Sellers called out.

I turned back, confused as to what he was saying. Sellers chuckled, gave a small shake of his head before he walked away himself. Had he known Asher would do this? Was that why he asked me to go out with him to begin with? And if so, why would he do that?

I stopped at Asher's truck and although it was unlocked, I didn't get inside. I waited. Just as I turned back to see if he was coming, I saw him headed toward me. Like before, he looked determined. His eyes locked on me. My cheeks heated up, again, the intensity of his eyes overwhelming me with trepidation. My body felt warm and I knew I was forgetting to breathe from the short rapid gasps coming from my mouth. I didn't know how to control my reaction to him.

When he got to me, I expected him to stop and open the door for me. Instead, the bag he carried in his hands dropped to the ground, his body crowding mine, as he pressed me up against his truck. Both his hands cupped my face before Asher Sutton's lips met mine. Hard yet soft, demanding yet tender, Asher tasted me like I was his last meal, and I was sure if he hadn't moved his hands to my hips and jerked me closer to him, I would have slid to the ground and blacked out. My legs were weak and my body trembled. Nothing had prepared me for this. Nothing had ever been this life altering. I felt like I was hit by a lightning.

And my world would never be the same after that.

chapter
SIX

Asher Sutton

MY BEDROOM REMAINED the same. It had once been the attic, but when I turned thirteen and got tired of sharing a bedroom with both Brent and Bray, I made a deal with Momma. If I cleaned out the attic and turned it into a bedroom, she would get me a window unit so I would have air in the summer when needed. For warmth, I ran a cheap ceramic heater.

It took a month, but when I had it all cleaned up, Momma kept her word. The other boys complained that I got my own room, but she reminded them I was the oldest.

When I'd moved out, no one tried to take it. I'd expected the twins to fight over it, but surprisingly they didn't. It was then that guilt tugged at me. Was it because they all hoped I would come back home?

I threw my duffel bag on the floor and sank down onto my bed. I missed home. I loved it here. I loved having my brothers around me, working the same land my father had worked. This was my life, or it had been, until the day it all came crashing down and changed everything forever.

I took the secret with me, but I wouldn't be able to keep it a secret any longer. Steel had to know. His heart would be broken for a while, but mine had been shattered beyond repair. Steel would survive this, he'd move on eventually. I had to believe that.

The nagging thought that Dixie had so easily fallen in love with someone else was driving me crazy. Just because I couldn't fill the void she'd left in my life didn't mean she shouldn't move on either. I wanted Dixie to be happy and knowing I was going to hurt her again, only made what I had to do even worse.

Heavy footsteps told me I had company. I was expecting Steel. I knew when I walked out of Jack's that he'd follow me home. Yes, I'd gotten jealous when he'd called Dixie "baby," but that wasn't why I'd left. The real reason was so fucked up that it hammered in my head and I knew I had to tell him. I couldn't sit back and watch this again. He had to know now.

Lifting my gaze from the floor, I met Steel's concerned yet determined expression. He was here to fight for her. To make sure I didn't ruin his chance with her. I had to tell him.

"I love her," my younger brother said, breaking the silence around us.

"She's easy to love," I replied.

Steel's lips tightened. He didn't want to feel as if he had to compete with me. "You crushed her and then you left her. Now she's mine, Asher, mine. I'll fight for her if you make me."

I stood and watched as Steel tensed up. Did he think I would hurt him? I'd protected him and beat the shit out of more than one bully over the years. He was my brother. I wanted him to be happy. Had letting Steel have Dixie been our only problem, I would have walked away and let them be happy. But that was not the problem, as much as I wished it were.

Walking over to a corner of the attic, I moved a loose board from the floor and bent down to retrieve an old shoe box. My world ended the day I discovered it three long years ago. Every good memory I'd had in my life up to that point had been centered around my Dixie. The contents of that box had taken all that away, ruining the memories, and leaving me a broken man.

I dusted it off because it hadn't been touched since the day I found it while moving some furniture around so that the bed wouldn't hit the squeaky board directly over the living room. I'd been making plans to sneak Dixie up here that weekend, but that never happened.

Sinking back down on my bed, I held the box with care. It caused me agony just to touch it knowing what was inside. There was no doubt or question that what it held was true. Looking up at Steel, I knew that I wasn't just going to end any hope he had of a future with Dixie, but that every memory he had of our father would also be altered forever. The same as mine had been.

"I never deserted her. Never stopped loving Dixie." I spoke, then lifted the lid. "Steel, I found this three years ago. I didn't intend to share it. But I also never planned on one of my brothers falling in love with my girl." I then shook my head. "She's not my girl. She can't be my girl." Reaching into the box, I removed the letters, the paper folded and unfolded so many times, the edges were worn from the handling. "This is why she can't be your girl either," I said, holding the letters out to my brother.

Steel was watching me with fear in his eyes, as if he'd understood the truth before he even looked inside. "What's this?" he asked, his voice shaky, unsure.

"It's the reason why I left her. The reason I can't have her. Why you can't have her either."

Steel opened the first letter. I couldn't watch him as he read it. I dropped my head into my hands and waited in silence. His world was going to be forever changed. Just as mine had been. And I was powerless to save him from the pain.

All the letters, but one, were written by Dixie's mother. In each she tells the man she is writing how much she loves and misses him. She begs him to take her away from her life so that they can start a new one together. The passion in her words would've been moving, if not for the fact that each and every one was addressed to my own father. A man I had once admired. A man whose name I had been proud to bear. A man I had mourned when he died. A man who'd deceived us all.

"This is . . ." Steel said with effort, before I felt the mattress sink beside me, as Steel sat down with a sigh. "I just can't . . ." he muttered and coughed.

"Keep reading," I told him as the acid in my throat burned.

I'd memorized the last letter she had written to him. Every word was branded on my brain.

Vance,

I won't keep writing these letters to you. Not if you're going to continue ignoring me. I don't agree with the words you said. I believe we can have happiness together. This child inside me deserves us both. It will be a part of you just as those boys are. You said you loved me. You said being with me made you feel young again. Complete. You said complete. But now, I'm carrying your child and you won't speak to me. Is it because she's pregnant again? I know she's your wife but I have a husband too. One I'm willing to walk away from. One I'm willing to leave for you.

Does that mean I love you more? Because I'm willing to tell him the truth? That I love you. That this child inside me is yours. Proof that the passion we have for each other is worthy of a chance.

I won't keep you from your boys. I know you love them as you should. But you don't love their mother. You love me. I know that.

Be with me, Vance. Fix the mistakes of our past. We messed up all those years ago by going our separate ways. My heart has been yours since I was fifteen. It will always be. Don't leave me. Don't turn your back on our child. That would destroy me.

I love you forever and always,

Millie

My father cheated on my mother.

Dixie was my sister.

The sickness slammed into me again, the words in that letter replaying in my head. I'd made love to Dixie. I'd been inside her and it was like heaven. I'd never experienced anything like it again. Yet, it had been sick and wrong.

"Did you show these to Mom?" Steel asked. His voice sounded strained. I understood what he was going through.

"No. And I never will," I replied, dropping my hands into my lap and looking over at my brother.

He was staring straight ahead at the wall with the letters clasped tightly in his hands. "He was a bastard. A lying bastard," Steel said, his pain heavy on each and every word, emphasizing what he was feeling.

"Yeah, he was," I replied. I wasn't going to argue that. He had also allowed another man to raise his child as his own. These letters were all dated months before Dixie's birth. Before Steel's. How could he do that? The final letter was one from my dad. It had erased any doubt I might have had about the truth. Dad claimed Dixie was his, but he'd said he loved us more. He wanted my mother and his boys. He couldn't leave us and he'd told her she needed to let him go. Her child would be Luke Monroe's. The man I knew to be Dixie's father.

There wasn't another letter after that. Not in this box at least. Dixie's mother had run off when Dixie was a toddler, leaving Luke to raise her alone. When Dixie had been five, Luke Monroe remarried a woman named Charlotte, who adored and cherished Dixie, eventually becoming the mother Dixie never had, and although Charlotte loved her fiercely, Dixie had always wondered about her birth mother, even planned on finding her one day. She longed to know why she had left her.

I never wanted her to find Millie Monroe. I hoped the woman was dead and had taken this secret with her to the grave. Dixie could never know. She'd had too much loss and pain in her life. It was why I'd suffered on my own. To protect her. Always to protect her.

"Why didn't you tell her?" Steel asked.

I turned to Steel, studied his face, the hurt and disbelief visible in his eyes, as he realized his world was slowly crumbling. But I also saw that he wasn't putting her first. He wasn't focused on protecting Dixie from this ugly secret.

"Because I would die to shield her from this kind of pain," I replied. Because I love her more than you ever could. I didn't say those last words aloud, but we both knew they were true.

"I can't tell her, can I, Asher? You aren't going to let me explain? I have to hurt her like you did?"

I stood and moved away from him. I needed some distance between us. He was thinking about himself first, and not her. That infuriated me the most. Steel had planned on making a life with her, yet he wasn't willing to sacrifice his happiness for Dixie's.

"The pain you'll cause her by breaking it off with her is nothing compared to the kind of pain . . . Steel, I made love to her. I've been inside her . . . took her innocence . . . and, dammit, I'm her brother! That's fucked with my head ever since . . . ripping me in two . . . sickening me . . . crushing me again and again. Because, I never stopped loving her."

Steel sat and stared at me silently. Several minutes passed as he mused. I waited for him to argue with me, but he didn't say a word.

Finally, he rose, and held the letters out to me. "I won't tell her. I won't tell anyone," he said, his voice thick with emotion. "I love her, too . . . fuck, this is sick. Does Luke not know? He's let us both date her. Hell, I've asked her to marry me."

I shook my head. "Of course he doesn't know. He woulda never let us date Dixie. This whole fucked up shit happened because the only two people who knew are now gone forever."

I took the letters and held them away from me, what they said so deplorable, it was hard to even grasp them. "How am I supposed to hurt her?" Steel sounded so torn. I'd been where he was. Wanting to explain it all to Dixie. Every time she looked at me with those big sad eyes, I wanted to tell her how much I loved her, but it was wrong, the entire thing twisted. This would only hurt her worse. She adored Luke Monroe. Not only would telling her mess her head up, but it would take away the security of knowing her daddy loves her. It would likely destroy Dixie.

"This will kill her, Steel. You know that," I said in a timid, lost voice.

He shook his head and then buried his face in both hands as we both stood there in silence. I understood what he was feeling. I'd lived it every day. Missing Dixie with every breath I took. This wasn't going to get easier for him. But Dixie would eventually heal and find happiness. That was all I had to hold onto. Knowing one day she'd get the life she deserved and all the fucking joy in the world. My girl belonged in the sunshine. This sick twisted darkness had been mine to suffer through, and now my brother would share it with me.

Steel turned to leave. I didn't stop him. I knew he needed time and space. Being alone was best for now. I stood there listening to his footsteps as he walked away from this room, these letters . . . knowing he would have to hurt her in order to save her from harm. Again, she'd suffer because of this sin, never knowing why it was happening.

"Be gentle with her! Please!" I yelled, unable to stop myself.

Steel paused at the top of the stairs. "Nothing about this is gentle. I don't know how I could be gentle."

Once I knew, I hadn't been able to even look at her. There were so many things I should've done differently. She deserved more from me than what I'd given her. "Hold her when she cries," I said. More than anything else I wished I'd done that, instead of just walking away and letting her suffer alone.

Four Years Ago . . .

KISSING DIXIE WAS the moment. That moment I didn't know could exist. But sitting in my truck outside my house after taking her home made me realize I'd finally found it. She was it. I didn't care about any other girls. Wasn't interested in ever touching another one again. Not after that kiss and the way she looked at me, the same thoughts and feelings I was experiencing reflected in the depths of her beautiful eyes.

Focusing on how right this felt was easier than thinking about the age difference. Or the fact her dad was probably going to beat my ass. Shooting me was also an option. But love made you crazy and fearless, and none of that seemed important to me right now.

The driver's side door jerked open. "What the fuck you sitting out here for? I got a piece of ass waiting on me and I need to go. Get out!" Bray's usual annoyed look was plastered on his face.

"It's past curfew," I pointed out.

"Yeah, well, Momma is in bed and you kept the motherfucking

wheels all evening. How am I supposed to go get some pussy if you've got the truck?"

"Jesus, Bray!" He had very little respect for females. A sex addict through and through. He was also insensitive and harsh. I wasn't sure why females loved him. Brent looked just like him, but was nice, kind, easy going. Yet, the women gravitated to Bray.

I got out of the truck and leaned close to smell him. Had to make sure he wasn't drinking.

"Get off me. I haven't had anything to drink."

"Just making sure. It's my job."

He laughed. "Ain't your motherfucking job. Hey, have you nailed Liza yet?"

I shook my head. I was taken. A smile slid across my face at the thought of kissing Dixie. What I felt was pure euphoria.

"Good. Don't like dipping my wick where you've already had your candle."

"Drive careful," I told him as the truck door closed. He was cranked up and pulling out before I even made it to the house.

Stepping into the kitchen, I saw Momma in her housecoat putting away the clean dishes. She glanced over her shoulder at me. "That hellion left, didn't he?" She asked, already knowing the truth.

"Yes, ma'am. He's gone. Bolted."

"He's gonna be my wild card. The one to make me go gray too soon."

"He thought you'd gone to bed."

She laughed. "No, he did not. Boy walked out that door knowing good and well I was in here washing the dishes. Son, that lie was for you. He better not knock some girl up. I'll make him raise the baby. I might not be able to do a lot with him, but I'll for sure make his ass be a daddy if he creates a life."

We all knew that to be true for all of us. Bray was careful. We all were. Had to be.

"Where've you been all evening?" she asked.

"With Dixie."

She put her towel down and turned around. "Well, it's about time. That poor girl has loved you long as I can remember. She's turned into a real beauty."

That surprised me. Not sure why. Nothing much ever got by Momma.

"She's young."

Momma shrugged. "Your daddy was five years older than me. We were just fine."

"Yeah, but you were seventeen when you started dating. Almost eighteen."

"Does she make you happy?"

"Yes," I replied.

"That right there is all that matters. You will be good to her. Treat her with respect and love her the way she deserves to be loved. That's what I know. That's what she knows. You do that and the rest will fall into place. Most of the time anyway."

"What about her dad?" I asked.

Momma chuckled. "Well, now you might have to run for cover before he takes a gun to you."

Great. Even Momma thought that might be the outcome.

"Oh, Asher, don't look so worried. Anything worth having comes with a price."

This time it was me who laughed. "My life may be the price."

She shrugged. "You got to figure out if she's worth that or not. I left you a plate in the microwave. Eat something and get your homework done." She kissed my cheek, then headed to the living room to watch her evening shows. She'd stay up until Bray got home. Then he'd get an earful, before doing it again tomorrow.

chapter
SEVEN

Dixie Monroe

STEEL HADN'T CALLED last night and he hadn't come by today. I could've gotten angry with him, but then again, yesterday I hadn't been able to put the ring he'd given me back on after taking it off. Before seeing Asher again, wearing that ring wasn't so hard. But now, it felt wrong. Like I was betraying Asher, even though he'd been the one to turn away from me.

I walked out to my car and glared down at the Sutton house. Why'd I let Asher affect me so much? Would I ever stop caring that he tossed me away after I gave him everything? I jerked the door of my red Jeep open while at the same time my phone started ringing. I stopped and pulled my phone from my pocket.

It was Steel.

Finally.

But I didn't want to answer.

It continued to ring. On the fourth ring, I gave in and said, "hello."

"Hey," he said, then paused. With just one word I knew

something was off. His tone was tense. Controlled. "We need to talk," he said on an exhale.

Asher. This was all because of Asher.

"Why? Did you talk to Asher? Is he not okay with . . . us?"

Steel didn't reply. His silence spoke volumes. This was about Asher. But why? Why did Asher care? And why was I letting a sliver of hope into my heart?

My knuckles turned white as I gripped the car door. He hadn't spoken to me in three years, yet he still managed to rip me to pieces every time he was back in town. I needed my closure, some form of finality between us so that I could move on.

"Fine, we'll talk later, but I have somewhere I need to be. I'll call you? Is that okay?" I said it not caring if it was okay or not. I wouldn't talk to Steel again until I found Asher first.

"Uh, okay, yeah," he replied, sounding nervous and uncertain.

"Good. I'll call you later." I quickly ended the call before he could say more. Climbing into my Jeep, I chose not to think about what I was going to say. If I did, I would've talked myself out of this. I turned my Jeep down the hill toward the Sutton house instead of going to town. Asher had been running from me long enough. He needed to face this once and for all. He needed to face us. What he did and what he threw away.

Steel's white truck was gone when I pulled around the house. I made my way to the barn. Asher's blue truck was parked where he had always parked it, just to the right of the pump house. He could see it from his bedroom window whenever he parked it there. That kept his brothers from sneaking off with it.

I stopped beside his truck and turned off my Jeep, but that was as far as I could get. Facing Asher was terrifying. His rejection and refusal to look at me had always felt like a knife plunging right through my heart. I needed a moment to mentally prepare. I knew I couldn't do this with him and walk away unscathed. I knew what lay in store for me afterwards.

The knock on my window startled me. Bray was standing there frowning. Taking one more deep breath, I closed my fingers around the metal latch, opening the door and stepping down.

"Steel ain't here, but then I'm guessin' you know that, seein' as how you're parked next to Ash."

Bray's tone held a warning. He thought I was here to cause trouble. I wasn't, not any more than Asher had caused when he drove into town and sent my heart into a tailspin again.

"Bray, it's past time I got some closure. Back off and let me go get it. He's had three years to get his head from his ass. Now I'm ready to move on and I need to finish this . . . thing . . . what was left unsaid between us . . . when it ended and your brother did the ending."

Bray stood there a moment, then sighed, stepping back so I could get past him. "You're right. This shit needs cleared up. Momma's gone with Brent to get some feed and some flowers for the front pots. Asher is . . ."

" . . . right here," he said, that deep familiar voice that still taunted me in my dreams interrupting Bray's. Asher had seen me drive up. I expected that. It's why I parked here. I wanted him to know I was coming.

"Fix this shit," Bray said, glaring at his older brother, before turning and walking away, leaving us standing there alone for the very first time in years.

I'd come to demand closure and now that I had his complete, undivided attention, I couldn't move a muscle. I couldn't form any words. I felt paralyzed. Asher stood a few feet away, only wearing a pair of worn jeans hung low enough on his hips that his v-cut lower oblique were in clear unhindered view. Where the hell was his shirt?

As if he could read my mind, the black cotton fabric of his tee shirt suddenly draped over all those muscles, the same muscles I used to think were made for sex, back when I was the one Asher was having sex with. Lifting my eyes, I took in his wet locks and freshly shaven face, realizing he'd just showered.

"You talked to Steel?" he asked, and my knees went weak. Why were my knees going weak? Why was being close to him like this as insanely all-consuming as it had been three long years ago? Before he tossed me out like trash.

"Not exactly. We're meeting up later to talk. Before I talked to him, I wanted to talk to you." It had taken all my strength to speak calmly. I wanted to scream at Asher. Demand to know why he hated me.

"You need to talk to Steel, not me," he replied, then he turned to walk away.

Just like before, he was blocking me out. Refusing to acknowledge me. I hated him again, how he used me, and then could so easily forget me. I hated that I still loved him. A scream tore loose and I lunged, grabbing Asher's arm to stop him. He wouldn't leave me again.

This time I wouldn't stand here and take it. I would tell him what a horrible person he was. I roared "no!" as my hands wrapped around his bicep, which once used to curl around my shoulder back when I was something precious to him. Pushing those memories aside, I squeezed his arm and jerked him toward me, as hard as I could.

Asher stopped. His body tensed. Asher Sutton was not a small guy. He was all hard lines and muscles. Broad shoulders with a narrow waist. Thighs that made women drool. Yet, here I was screaming at him, and yanking on his arm like a kid, throwing a temper tantrum.

"Not this time! You won't walk away from me again!" I tried to fill my voice with determination but I was fighting back tears inside.

Asher slowly turned. I let his arm go, suddenly realizing I was touching him. When his eyes met mine, I was unprepared for the pain I saw in them. It took my breath away and I had to take a step back to recover.

"Haven't I done enough?" he replied. "Can't this be all I have to endure? Do you want me to continue killing us both? Reduce us both to nothing?"

He didn't try to hide his pain, that hateful mask of relaxed indifference he'd used with me for so long now replaced by unchecked, raw anguish. It took all I had in me to stop myself from taking him into my arms, to make that look in his eyes go away.

"Why? I need to know why," I spoke softly. I stood where I was because I knew Asher would push me away if I went to him. He wouldn't let me touch him. There was too much emotion running through him.

"I can't be who you need me to be. I can't be who you deserve me to be. I thought once that I could, but I found out that I made a terrible mistake. One I can't take back." He tightly closed his eyes, muttered a curse, before opening them again and leveling them on me. "If I could erase the past, our time together, I would take it all back. Every single moment, Dixie. I would wipe out every goddamn moment. Then you could move on and forget me. You were never meant to belong to a Sutton boy."

Four Years Ago . . .

A WEEK HAD passed since he first kissed me. Walking out my front door every single morning to find Asher Sutton standing at his truck, with his arms crossed and that smile on his face, still seemed unreal to me. Like I was living in a dream. But it wasn't a dream. This was real. I was Asher Sutton's . . . girlfriend? I then realized I wasn't sure I should call myself that. We hadn't discussed it yet.

He kissed me. He walked me to my classes. Had me wait on him until practice was over so he could drive me home. But we didn't go anywhere together. He wasn't asking me out on dates. Maybe I was making more of this than was actually there. My heart sank at the mere thought I'd been imaging all this.

"Mornin'," Asher said as I reached him. He always waited leaning back against the passenger side of the truck.

"Good morning," I replied, trying to smile. The joy I'd felt at stepping outside and seeing Asher was quickly fading. Maybe I was misunderstanding this thing between us.

Asher took a step closer. His hand cupped my face. "What's wrong? I'm used to seeing a smile. Not a big fan of that frown."

I tried harder to force a smile.

"Dix, that ain't a real smile," was his response.

I shrugged my shoulders. "Guess I'm not awake yet. Stayed up too late reading."

He didn't look convinced, but he bent his head and pressed a kiss to my temple, looking behind me before moving back. "Not brave enough to kiss you the way I like with your daddy watching us. I can see his figure in the window."

That did make me smile a little. I knew Asher was being funny because Daddy wouldn't be standing in the window. Then again, he was probably watching from somewhere.

Asher opened the truck door and held out his hand. Like I always did, I slipped my hand in his and climbed into the truck. This part was real. He was here taking me to school. I should be happy about this. I was being greedy wanting more.

When he was inside, he patted the seat right next to him. "Why don't you slide over here?"

I moved my book bag to the floorboard and slid over a little. This was a first.

"You know I don't bite, Dix. Come on, get closer, up against me."

I continued to slide over until Asher's hand rested on my left knee. "There. That's better. I like that."

I agreed, it was better. Much better.

"I got my smile back," he said, sounding pleased with himself. "Tell me what you were reading last night."

I didn't imagine that Asher was a reader. "Lord of the Flies for literature class. I have to write a report on it."

Asher nodded. "I remember that. My favorite book we read that year was The Old Man and the Sea."

"That's next month's required reading."

"You'll have to tell me what you think of it."

This conversation wasn't one that people in a relationship had. Or was it? I had no idea. But I was sitting beside him with his hand on my knee, which was making my heart beat faster. I knew that had to mean something.

"After the game tonight, will you go with me to Jack's? The team will be there because the food is free. I'd like to have you with me."

That was a date. He was asking me on a date. Daddy wouldn't let me go inside Jack's. But I wasn't going to worry about that. I would do it anyway and hope Jack didn't tell, which was obviously a friggin' long shot.

"Okay," I agreed.

He squeezed my knee. "Good. I'm glad."

To me, it was more than good. It was wonderful. Stupendous. Groundbreaking. Even though I could end up being grounded for the rest of my life. It was the best thing that ever happened to me.

When he pulled into his parking spot at school, I could see people, mainly girls, turning to watch his truck approach. They saw me sitting there close to him. Not a single female looked happy. It wasn't my first day arriving in his truck, but it was the first time I ever rode right beside him.

He parked the truck, leaned down, until his lips captured mine. He then kissed me. Really kissed me. The toe curling kind of kiss that made you forget to breathe. My right hand reached up to grab his shoulder. His face tilted and the kiss deepened. The minty taste of his toothpaste was the most delicious thing I'd ever had touch my tongue.

A banging noise stopped us and Asher sighed, pulling back just a little so that he could look directly into my eyes. "Ignore them. Anything they say. Especially Bray. He's a smartass."

Before the last word left his mouth, Asher's door was jerked open. Bray and Brent Sutton were standing there grinning like we were the funniest thing they'd ever seen.

"I'm tired of having to get a fucking ride to school. You can do this shit with us in the truck. Dix don't care, do you, Dix? Hell, I'll even drive and you two can suck face the entire way to school." Bray Sutton was dangerous, sexy and dark. Very different from his friendly, good-natured twin. You'd think they were born on different continents, if they didn't look exactly alike.

"Move out of the fucking way," Asher snarled.

"I'm serious, I'll drive and make comments. We can throw the other three dipshits in the back and let them air. You two can then go at it. Just give me a warning before any sexy shit starts. I might have to pull over and watch."

"Jesus! Shut the hell up!" Asher yelled, reaching over to squeeze my hand. "I'm sorry, Dixie, but you already know there's not an excuse for him. He has no filter."

I was smiling. Giggling, really. These boys had been in my life for as long as I could remember. I knew them all. Every single one. Though I'd only loved Asher from the start.

"It's okay," I assured him.

Asher briefly kissed my lips. He got out of the truck, pushing Bray back, then held out his hand for me.

"Always knew it would be you two. Steel makes more sense, but she only noticed you. Ain't that right, Dix?" Brent asked, with his friendly smile in place.

I blushed and Asher pulled me against him. "If you two assholes don't leave my girl alone, you'll all be walking to school."

They went back and forth with each other. I could hear them, but *their words weren't registering at all. Nothing mattered. Nothing but the fact that Asher Sutton had just called me his girl. I didn't stop smiling all day.*

chapter
EIGHT

Asher Sutton

HER BEAUTIFUL FACE crumpled from my words and I hated myself for that. I hated the air that I breathed. That all I knew how to do was hurt her. When all I wanted was to cherish Dixie. Love her. Make her happy.

"No," she said, shaking her head. "No," she repeated, tears flowing freely down her face. "I don't believe that. You're pushing me away. Trying to hurt me again. I won't listen to you. You're lying. This hurts you, too. I just can't figure out why you're doing this. Why you're destroying us both." She then took a step toward me. I took a step back. I didn't trust myself that close to her. I wanted to wrap her up in my arms. Tell her everything would be okay, which I knew it would never be.

"Please, tell me. Tell me why you left me. At least give me that, Asher. I gave you *everything* and you threw it all away like it meant nothing to you. I loved you and you just used me and left me. You were the only man I wanted. I thought we were forever. You said we were forever. That you would never want anyone else.

That I was everything to you." She was crying uncontrollably now.

"*You were!*" I roared. I couldn't stand here any longer and let her keep believing she'd meant nothing to me. I knew I let her down. I knew I'd crushed her. I knew all that. But this had to end. "You were it for me. Dammit, Dixie, you probably always will be. But we can't be. There are things you don't know that make anything between us impossible. Things I won't tell you, things I'll take to the grave because I can't hurt you anymore. I did hurt you and I'm sorry. I will be sorry for the rest of my life. But you'll move on and fall in love with a guy who can love you back. Stay with you forever." I paused as Steel's white truck came around the house. He had to face her now. This had to be finished and done. "And Steel can't love you either."

"Steel loves me," Dixie replied, her voice cracking again.

"Of course he does. Anyone that gets a chance to know you loves you almost immediately. You're . . . you . . . Dix. You're you." I was going to say too much. I stopped talking and clenched my teeth as Steel parked his truck and climbed out. He looked pale. Like he'd been sick. He had to be stronger than this. Facing this shit was something no one should ever suffer. But we had to, thanks to the man we once thought hung the moon. He'd left behind a legacy of lies. One that would leave me soulless and hollow for the rest of my life.

"Steel, what's wrong?" Dixie asked. The concern in her voice made me jealous. I was being ridiculous, Dixie was my sister, and I was still being jealous over her. This disgusting, twisted, unfair life that our father had thrown our way was so fucking insane, I still couldn't wrap my mind around it.

I could sense Steel looking for help. I couldn't do this for him. He had to end it. Send her away. "Remember what I said," I told him, hoping that he understood. I wanted him to hold her when she broke.

"I can't," he responded, shaking his head. I wasn't sure what he meant. What was it that he couldn't do? Steel couldn't stay with her. He knew that.

"Dixie, you're our sister." The words fell from his lips before I could register in my head exactly what he meant. He just said it. Steel just told her.

I heard her gasp and as if in slow motion, I watched as confusion filled her eyes when Dixie turned and looked back at me. I had to fix this. He couldn't do it this way. Not to Dixie. She'd never recover. He was going to ruin her too. She'd be as empty as I'd become.

"Your mom . . ." Steel said as I yelled, "no," stopping my brother from saying anything else. Why had I trusted him? What the fuck had I been thinking? I'd given him the power to hurt my Dixie. "Don't do this," I told him, as I moved quickly toward Steel. " . . . had an affair with our dad," he finished. The words were the last thing that came out of his mouth before my fist slammed into his jaw, knocking him back against his truck. If it had been anyone other than my brother, I would've continued to pummel him senseless, until he blacked out, or until he couldn't speak anymore.

I stood above him as he grabbed his jaw, glaring up at me. "She deserved to know," he said, his slurring from the impact noticeable.

"She didn't deserve this. No one deserves this," I replied, shaking my head.

"Asher?" Dixie's soft voice came from behind me and I tensed having to face her.

"Fucking tell her. She knows now. Finish it," Steel said, remaining on the ground, holding his swelling face.

A hand touched my arm softly and I winced. I didn't want Dixie to touch me. I couldn't stand the memory of that. When she grabbed me before, I felt her anger. That was okay, but her gentle touch was something I couldn't bear right now. I said, "Dixie, you don't want to hear this," unable to turn around and face her.

"Yes, I do," she replied.

"Don't, Dix. Just leave. Run like hell and don't come near us again. Go home to that house up there and let your daddy hold you tight. Remind yourself you're loved and you deserve a fairytale. Not what you'll get down here. We can't give you . . . anything. Not a fucking thing," I spoke, then backed away, not wanting to look in her eyes.

"Is he telling the truth? Did your . . . am I . . ." she trailed off, her voice turning into a whisper.

"Our sister Dixie. You're our sister." Steel spoke and again I charged him. Two arms wrapped around mine, jerking me back. "Don't. He's right. This shit is something she needs to hear, Asher. It's her life too," Bray said. His voice was strained as I pulled against his hold, wanting to shut Steel up. "Can't believe you kept this goddamn shit to yourself," Bray said, pain etched in his words.

"Go home, Dixie. Please," I begged her, before Steel could say anything more.

She shook her head and backed away unsteadily. Her face had paled and I realized that driving probably wasn't safe.

"Wait, don't drive. Not like this. I'll drive you and I'll walk back." I then yanked my arms free.

"How do you know?" she asked.

Telling Dixie anything more would only hurt her further. The people who'd conceived her both then abandoned her. This was all much worse for her than it could ever be for us. Didn't Steel understand that? She was losing so much more. I wanted Dixie to live the life I couldn't give her, the one I'd planned on, where she never doubted how special or loved she was. I just shook my head, refusing to give her any answers.

"How?" Dixie asked again, staring at me with a pleading look in her eyes. The light in those eyes that I loved seeing was completely snuffed out now. Steel had destroyed her soul. I would never be able to forgive him. "You won't tell me anything. How do I even know this isn't some stupid mistake? Who told you this, Asher?"

If I told her about the letters, she would demand that I show her. I didn't want this touching Dixie any more than it already had. I preferred letting her walk away, without believing a word. "Go home to your daddy," I repeated.

"He found letters from your mom to our dad. Under a floorboard in the attic three years ago. He didn't tell anyone because he thinks he's protecting you," Steel said, now standing again, his eyes remaining on me.

Bray's hand clamped down on my shoulder. "She deserves to know this, too. Stop trying to protect her, Asher."

"Letters? You have letters?" she asked, her eyes glistening with new tears. "You have letters saying that my daddy isn't my father? That you . . ." she stopped and covered her mouth, unleashing a sob that shredded me. Rocked me through to the core. Her knees buckled and I started to move toward her, but Bray stopped me, moving instead. "No, I got her," he said. I let him go, he loved her too, but he loved her the way a brother should.

Bray pulled her into his arms. He held her as she tucked her head under his chin and sobbed. That was all that I'd wanted. Someone to hold her the way she needed it.

"She deserved to know," Steel said, reminding me that he was still here.

"No one deserves this," I replied, before turning and walking to my truck. I had to leave, I couldn't stay here, watching Dixie fall apart. Just when I thought I couldn't hurt any more, I was again proven wrong. Knowing that Dixie would now live this nightmare was more than I could handle.

Four Years Ago . . .

"ARE YOU REALLY dating Dixie?" Steel asked, as he reached the top of the stairs leading up to my attic bedroom. I'd always wondered if Steel liked Dixie. After all, they were the same age, she was beautiful, kind and smart. Why wouldn't he like her? He should. Part of me hoped he would. Then I could stop feeling guilty about wanting a girl three years younger than me and that I had no business being with.

"Yeah," I replied, picking up my duffel bag that had my clean uniform in it for the game later on tonight. "You good with that?" I wasn't sure why I asked. If he wasn't, it wouldn't change anything. He'd had years to show interest in Dixie. Years. He'd missed his chance.

He didn't respond right away. He needed to get to the fieldhouse. He was a freshman and wasn't starting, but he'd be taking my place next year. He had to act like my backup and be ready. "She's a freshman, Asher. You're going off to Florida next year."

Steel was stating the obvious. I calmly responded to my brother, "and when that time gets closer, Dix and I will deal with that like we should."

"She's okay with you leaving?"

Sighing, I grabbed my hat and put it on. "Look, if you like Dixie, you had years to show it. To do something. You never did. Once she turned fifteen, things changed for me. For us. She likes me, just as much as I like her. You can't go getting weird about it now. Your time is up. Let's get to the fieldhouse. Brent and Bray are already in the truck."

He turned and headed back down the stairs. His frowning eyebrows told me he wasn't done with this. I figured we'd have it eventually. Steel was quieter than me. He was more studious and thought things over before he spoke. This would be no different. The horn on the truck then began to blare. Momma spoke to warn against the time, "better get out there. Y'all gonna be late," she said as we walked into the kitchen. "Play hard. I'll be watching." She said the same thing every Friday night. And we all loved to hear it.

"Yes, ma'am," we replied in unison. I kissed her cheek then headed for the door. I knew Steel would do the same.

"You taking Dixie to Jack's after the game?" Momma called out behind me.

"Yes ma'am," I replied.

"You talked to Luke about that?"

"Yes, ma'am."

"Good. Didn't want to hear you'd been shot by the neighbor. That would be inconvenient."

Smiling, I left the house, pushing thoughts of my brother, Dixie and her father back and away from the game. My focus had to be there. We were undefeated. I had to keep it that way. It was my responsibility.

"Get your asses out here! I don't want to run sprints after the fucking game because the two of you ran us late!" Bray yelled. He was right. I didn't want to run sprints either. "We better hurry," I told Steel, as I broke into a run. We tossed our bags into the bed of the truck beside Brent, Steel climbing in back with him. Bray was sitting on the passenger's side. We had taken our usual seats. Next year, it would be Dallas in the back and Brent and Bray in the front. I'd be off at college. The thought made me sad.

Dixie would be ten hours away. My life here would consist of holidays and a few short weeks in the summer. Steel was right. I had the rest of the school year. What if Dixie got tired of her boyfriend never being around? I'd lose her. She'd move on.

Fuck. I couldn't think about that right now. I had a game. I'd think about it later. There had to be an answer. We hadn't had enough time together, and losing her wasn't an option.

chapter
NINE

Dixie Monroe

FOR THREE YEARS, I'd wanted answers. Countless nights, I'd lain in bed, thinking that just knowing Asher still loved me would've made everything okay. That was all that mattered. Nothing could hurt more than Asher not loving me anymore.

I'd been wrong.

So very wrong.

"Come on, Dix. Let's take you home," Bray said, as we began moving toward my Jeep. Home. My home. Was it still my home? Did Daddy know this? Did he love me anyway? Could I tell him? How could I tell him?

"Does my daddy know?" I asked Bray.

He reached around me and opened the passenger's door. "I didn't even know. So I'm not sure who knew, but it won't make a difference to your daddy. He loves you and has loved you all your life. In his heart, you're his little girl. That's something I'm fucking positive about."

I let Bray help me up into the Jeep. I felt as if I was walking through fog. Nothing made sense. My bearings were destroyed. I'd watched as Asher's truck drove away, but I never saw Steel leave. I couldn't look at him now, he'd been the one I hoped could eventually heal me, but he'd just made it all worse.

"Why would he keep this from me?" I asked, staring out the window at the field of hay, the birds moving, dipping, enjoying themselves, while I was trapped in hell.

"Because since you were a kid he's protected you. He'd do anything to protect you, Dixie. It wasn't the right decision, but it was because he loves you. He's suffered alone for three years with this and all because he loves you. He didn't want you to know it. He wanted you happy. You can't completely fault him for that."

He wanted me happy? He'd broken my heart. How was that making me happy? "He can't love me. His actions prove different."

Bray sighed and cranked the Jeep. "His love ain't normal when it comes to you. Never was," he replied. "But don't doubt that he loves you, Dixie. Damn, he smashed in our little brother's face because he was trying to protect you. Asher's never hit one of us. We've hit each other and he's broken it up, but he's always brought it to a halt. He picked you over Steel. That's fucking huge. Be mad at him for not telling you, but don't think he doesn't love you."

I couldn't listen to this. He was my brother. Asher was my brother. The horror of that washed over me, a wail filling the Jeep as I curled into a ball and allowed the sorrow to consume me.

Four Years Ago . . .

ASHER STOOD WITH his arm around me as he laughed at Brent mocking Bray, the two battling it out over pool. I was at Jack's after a game. At Jack's and I was with Asher. This was another daydream I'd repeatedly played in my head so many times, I had a hard time now believing it was happening. That I was here with him, my daddy knew about it, and everything was okay. Asher went to see him after school, before he'd gone to the fieldhouse to prepare for their game. He'd talked to daddy and promised him I'd be safe and with him at all times. When daddy agreed to let me go, I threw myself at him, hugging him tightly and thanking him right there in front of Asher. I'd expected him to say no. But Asher was good with people. Everyone liked and trusted him.

"You want another Coke?" Asher asked me.

"No, thanks. I'm good," I replied.

He pressed a kiss to my temple and whispered, "If you're bored, we can go."

As if I could ever be bored with Asher Sutton. "I'm enjoying myself. This is the first time I've ever been in the front of Jack's. Daddy always made me pick up the food in the back."

Asher chuckled. "I know. I've seen you more than once through that door over there."

"And I've also seen you," I replied. I'd been looking for him. I knew he was in here. I'd seen his truck. But that sounded stalkerish, so I kept that information to myself.

Andrea James then cooed, "Hey, Asher, you were amazing tonight," sauntering up to him, and pressing her body against his as if I wasn't standing right there next to him. "I have a special treat for you. Want to leave this party?"

Asher tightened his hold around me, scooting closer, and moving back from Andrea. "I'm here with Dix. I thought that was obvious."

Andrea finally looked at me, as if she hadn't realized I was there. "Oh, I didn't think you'd be with her. Asher, she's a freshman."

"I'm aware of that and yes, I'm with her."

Andrea smirked. "Okay then. When you get tired of babysitting, you know my number."

When she turned to walk off, Asher looked down at me. "She's a bitch. The crazy kind. Sorry about that, Dixie."

"And Asher never tapped that ass. He's smarter than that," Bray said, a little too loudly for my taste. "But I might now that Asher's off the market."

"You know he's an idiot, right?" Asher said with an apologetic smile. "But he's right. I'm off the market."

I laughed. It felt right. Being with Asher. Laughing at his brothers. I'd grown up with the Sutton boys. This fit. Made sense.

As for Andrea James, Asher would get a lot of that kind of attention in his life. I could get jealous every time it happened or accept it for what it was. The way Asher had kept his arm around me and dealt with her made it easier for me to handle, giving me no reason to feel insecure. He was beautiful and women loved him, but now he was mine.

"Don't worry about her sister either. He won't be going after Emily James' ass. After Asher set her straight for doing that shit to you, he wrote her off. Hell, we all did. She messed with our Dixie," Brent said, winking and smiling at me, like I knew this had happened.

I tilted my head back and looked up at Asher, who was glaring at his brother. "You made Emily stop?"

He sighed then nodded. "Yeah."

"How did you know it was her?"

"Asked a few questions," he responded. "Didn't want you suffering anymore."

There was no possible way for me not to love Asher. He owned my heart. I stepped to his front, wrapped my arms around his neck, and held him tight. "Thank you," I said. "You're my hero."

"Hey, I threatened her, too," Bray called from across the pool table.

"She's not hugging you. Back the hell off," Asher returned as he hugged me back.

If my life could always be this perfect, I never wanted it to end. There'd be no one for me but Asher. I was young, but that I knew. When your soul finds its match, there's no doubt in your heart. Telling Asher I loved him right now was too soon, I knew I had to wait. So as much as

I wanted to pepper his face with kisses and tell him how I felt, I didn't. Instead, I let him turn me in his arms and hold me against his chest. I would have been happy to stay there forever.

chapter
TEN

Steel Sutton

ASHER HADN'T COME home last night. Bray and Brent went to look for him and came back after two in the morning with no sign of our big brother. Momma was going to notice that he wasn't here. Keeping his disappearance from her would be hard. I could smell the bacon now and knew we'd have a big breakfast waiting on us.

I believed I'd done the right thing. Dixie needed to know. It was wrong to keep that kind of thing from her. Why couldn't Asher see that? I wouldn't desert her the way he had, but she needed to know the reason we couldn't be together anymore.

One day Dixie would've found out the truth on her own and we wouldn't have been there to help. She planned on finding her real mother at some point. She didn't need to be blindsided by some bitch who didn't love her anyway.

And nothing had changed for me. I loved her as much as before and I wasn't sure those feelings would ever go away.

"His bed's still empty," Brent said, as he walked into my room.

"Truck's gone, too. But his shit is still here," Dallas added, following Brent. He'd gotten up early to go work out in the barn. It was his normal morning routine.

"Momma ain't gonna be happy about this. What're we gonna tell her?" I asked, looking to Bray for an answer. He shook his head and walked over to the window. "Hell if I know. Can't tell her the truth. It would kill her dead on the floor."

"Sure didn't matter to Steel that it might kill Dix like that." Dallas said it like I wasn't in the room. He just glared in my direction. He'd been pissed at me when he realized Asher had kept it from Dixie to protect her and I had told her anyway. Dallas thought Asher could do no wrong. He didn't remember our dad because he was too young when dad died. Asher had always been the oldest male in his life, his onlyrole model.

"Dixie needed to know," Bray said, looking back at Dallas.

"Really? Cause you want to keep it from Momma, to protect her just like Asher wanted to protect Dixie," Dallas quickly shot back. He was two inches taller than Bray and his shoulders were wider and stronger, but we still saw him as the baby of the family. And even though no one else in Malroy messed with Dallas, we still treated him as the youngest.

"Shut up, Dallas! You don't understand."

"The *fuck* I don't! I understand Asher told that dipshit a secret and trusted him to keep it from Dixie. And he didn't do it," Dallas accused, pointing at me.

"Take it down a notch or ten," Brent said as he walked into the room, squinting against the sunlight streaming in from the window. He was still in his flannel pajama pants, his blond hair sticking up in several directions. He rarely went without a shirt, still hiding the tattoo on his waist from Momma because he didn't want to deal with what she'd say. Brent was the last one of us anyone expected to get a tattoo. The word "yesterday" was inked on his right hip bone and no one knew what it meant. Except possibly Bray, because those two communicated without words. Their twin bond was fucking freakish at times.

Bray drawled, "sleeping beauty, glad you could join us."

"Y'all woke me up. I bet Momma heard y'all, too," Brent grumbled, flopping back on Dallas's bed, which was unmade and torn to pieces. "And for the record, I think it was a shit thing to do for you to tell her that," Brent added, lifting his head from the pillow to look at me with disgust, before dropping it down and leaving it.

"Majority vote is you suck," Dallas said.

Bray groaned and turned around to shoot an angry glare at his brothers. "It's done. Shut up and let it go. Now she knows and Asher has got to get a fucking grip. We can't let him fall off the deep end. He was pretty damn close before this happened. He's carried this shit around on his own for three fucking years. Remember that. Our goal is to find him. Not sit here and discuss if Steel did the right thing or not."

I glanced down at my phone. Dixie hadn't texted me. I'd almost expected something from her. We'd been fucking engaged . . . well, nearly. Now we were related. My stomach turned again. The only thing keeping me from losing my shit was the fact we hadn't had sex. We had come close, but she always put the brakes on. As pissed as I was getting, I'm damn sure glad she did. Asher had to live knowing he'd slept with her. And that he'd taken her damn virginity. Fuck . . . I couldn't imagine that.

"I can't imagine what he's been dealing with. Three years of daily hell. All I want to do is go drink so much I can't feel a motherfucking thing." Bray's scowl deepened and he headed for the door. "Fuck drinking, I'm going to find him," he said, before leaving us all sitting there, watching him exit the room.

"Guess that leaves us to explain their absence. Momma's

BOYS *south of the* MASON DIXON   83

gonna love this," Dallas said, moving toward the door himself.

"I should go with him," Brent added, sitting up and scratching his head. He wasn't a morning person and Bray had looked like a man on a mission.

"You'll be in his way, and he'll be gone before you can slide into a pair of jeans anyway. Let him go, you go charm Momma with pretty boy." I spoke, nodding my head for him to follow Dallas.

Brent agreed with a tilt of his chin and then left the room, hopefully planning to find a shirt first before he joined Momma and Dallas in the kitchen.

chapter ELEVEN

Asher Sutton

THIS MORNING AT seven, I'd been sitting in my truck parked behind the football field, when I got a text from Dixie. She asked me where I was. I stared at my phone for ten minutes before responding. She didn't need to ask me why I was here because she knew. Here, I felt safe. The place was deserted, with school being out, and it was the only place I could think of where I could park and be left alone.

Half an hour later, the passenger side of my truck opened and Dixie climbed in. She didn't knock but I was expecting her. I knew she'd come, but then again, I knew Dixie better than anyone else. Better even than Steel.

Steel.

I loved him, but I couldn't be trusted to be around him right now.

"You been here all night?" Dixie asked.

"Yeah," I muttered.

"You sleep any?"

"Nope. Not a wink."

I hadn't been able to close my eyes. I wanted to, needing the escape, even for the briefest of moments, but I couldn't, not when all I saw when I closed my eyes was Dixie sobbing in Bray's arms. Then I had to fight the urge to go find Steel and beat the shit out of him for doing this to her.

"Bray came by late last night. He was looking for you."

I'd ignored all their texts and calls. My phone was on silent, wanting to sit here alone and think, knowing I wouldn't find peace. They wanted to make sure that I was alright because they worried about me, but I hadn't been alright.

"I was mad at you yesterday. I hated you for a moment. For not telling me. For keeping it from me." Her soft voice cut right through me. I knew she hated me and had reasons. But hearing it from her lips wasn't easy.

"I know," I managed to croak through the emotion clogging my throat.

"I get it. I thought about it all last night. I understand, I do," she said, then her hand touched mine and I flinched, the contact unsettling, confusing.

"Just wanted to protect you," I replied, needing Dixie to know that I never meant to hurt her and I'd do anything not to hurt her again.

"I know that now . . . everything . . . I let myself remember it all. Stuff I'd blocked out because it was too painful, I remembered it all last night. How you used to be with me . . . how we used to be together . . . how sure I was you would love me forever. Then you just turned away without a word. I never understood how you could do that to me. It haunted me. I loved you . . . I loved you so much . . . but you also loved me, too. It's why you did it. I get it. I understand now."

Fuck, this was hard, it was past time we did this, but still, it was brutal. The familiar smell of coconut and honey filled the cab of the truck. It had been so long since I'd been close enough to Dixie to smell her scent. It reminded me of how good she'd felt in my arms, how soft her skin was, like satin, warm satin. And how when I sank into her, molded to her body, nothing had been that perfect. The pleasure on her face had made my heart pound just to possess her. She was mine. Back then, all mine.

"I can't do this . . . you . . . I need you to leave. Please. Being this close to you . . . I'm not ready for that. I don't think I'll ever be. My heart doesn't seem to understand I can't have you . . . that it's fucking impossible. Please, Dixie." I sounded desperate. I couldn't look at her. I needed her to go.

Dixie moved, but she didn't open the door. Instead, she scooted closer to me, her smell making me light headed. Fuck, she had to get out.

"Dix," I warned, gripping the steering wheel.

"I'll leave, but first, would you hold me?"

How did I tell her no? And how would I let her go if I allowed myself to touch her again?

"Please, Ash? Hold me this once. I need this."

I learned a long time ago that I would do anything, sell my soul for this girl if needed. Now she was a woman and it was no different, so I released my death grip on the steering wheel and rested my arm on the seat. Dixie cuddled against me, then laid her head on my chest. Closing my arms around her, I inhaled deeply, letting her warmth fill my senses one final time. We didn't have a goodbye. I didn't give us one. She was right, this was the end, the one we'd needed back then, but I hadn't been ready to give it to her.

"I think I'll always love you. I can't help that," she said quietly.

I knew I'd always love her, but telling her that right now would only hurt her more. Dixie had to move on and find that ray of sunshine in her life, the one I knew she belonged in. A man who would love her unconditionally, give her a home, happiness and children. He'd make her dreams come true. He'd treat her like a princess and if he didn't, I'd make him wish he was never born.

I would never have a wife. I couldn't do that to someone. My heart has belonged to the very same girl since I was sixteen years old. No amount of lies and sin could take that away from me. What I felt for Dixie was pure. Simple truth, one I didn't want to change. I'd watch her live her life from afar and make sure it was everything she wanted, everything Dixie deserved.

When I didn't respond, she didn't say any more. We sat there for an hour, I held her in my arms one last time and tried to memorize every moment of it. I made plans in my head to make sure that I righted every wrong done to her. It was the only thing keeping me sane.

The sound of tires on gravel and Bray's diesel engine suddenly broke us apart. Dixie moved over, opened the truck door and stepped out without saying a word. We'd said all there was to say. I watched her as she walked to her Jeep. She didn't acknowledge Bray. Instead, she climbed inside and drove away.

I waited for Bray to come to me. Obviously, he'd found me. I was surprised it took him so long to think about this spot, but I was thankful it took some time. When I saw him approaching my door, I rolled down the window and exhaled.

"Y'all talk about it?" Bray asked with a scowl.

"She got her closure," I said, equaling his scowl with one of my very own.

"Been looking for your ass all morning and also most of last night. Momma's cooked a big breakfast."

I cranked the truck. "Not sure I'm ready to see Steel."

Bray sighed. "He thought she should know. Maybe she did. The girl never moved on. The way you left it wasn't an ending for her. She wasn't healing. The wound was still open."

"She was engaged to Steel," I reminded him. Dixie had moved on. Put me behind her. Was going to marry my brother.

"Shit. She hadn't even said yes. I don't think she would've been able to until she saw you again. No point discussing that now. We'll never know."

Dixie was going to be okay. Her daddy would reassure her. She'd find a man to love her. I had to believe in that.

"Let's go home and eat before Momma comes looking for the both of us."

With a nod I said, "See you there," and dropped the truck into first.

Three Years Ago . . .

THERE WAS NO age difference. At least it felt that way to me. I loved Dixie. I loved being with her. I loved the way her laugh could make whatever shit I was dealing with better. Other girls had never done that for me. Momma said that the way I looked at Dixie was the way Dad looked at her. It was how she knew he was the one and that there'd never be anyone else for him. I felt that way about Dixie.

As the months began to pass and spring drew closer, I knew I would have to make some decisions about my future. I wanted to sign with Florida, but I couldn't leave her. My life was with Dixie and abandoning her to go to college wasn't what I wanted. Football wasn't my future. It was a way to pay for school. I could get another scholarship somewhere closer. Momma said as long as I used my talent to get my schooling paid for, she didn't care where I chose to go. I just needed a good education.

Telling Dixie all this, however, was going to be the difficult part. I'd hinted about staying around, close to her, and she'd always said, "no, you belong in a big fancy college. You love football. I want that for you." What she didn't understand was that I loved her more. She was my future. Not playing football.

I pulled into her drive and she was already outside on the porch doing something, wearing a pair of cut-off jeans and a brightly colored tee shirt. Her feet were bare, but she ran down the stairs, stepping through the grass until she reached me, my heart swelling with joy and pleasure, so damn big it shouldn't fit inside my chest. This, was all I wanted. Dixie was my nirvana.

"I wasn't expecting you for another hour. I'm not dressed yet," she said with a smile.

"I got off early," I replied. My shifts at the grocery store were late only on weekend nights. On school nights, I left at seven. Tonight they'd let me go at five thirty because things had been so slow. Everyone was at home eating dinner and the streets of the town were usually empty as a desert by now.

"Are you tired? We don't have to go to Jack's."

I wasn't tired, but I didn't want to go to Jack's either. I wanted Dixie to myself. "I could let Bray and Brent take the truck when they get off work. We could walk down to the lake."

"I could go pack us dinner. Momma cooked plenty meatloaf. I haven't eaten yet," Dixie offered.

"That sounds better than a bar full of people."

Smiling, she stood on her tip toes. "You go drop the truck off at your house for the boys and I'll go pack us a picnic."

"Deal," I replied against her lips. It was getting harder and harder not to do more than just kiss, touching and kissing here and there. I wanted it all, but until she was ready, I was happy with what we did do.

I watched as she ran to the house. Her ass was too damn perfect in those shorts. I'd seen it up close and personal two weeks ago when she'd finally let me kiss my way between her legs. That had been an experience she was happy to repeat and we'd done it a lot since then. Laughing to myself, I climbed back in my truck and headed to the house.

Bray and Brent both worked at Norton Knolls' stables. The Knolls raised and trained, then sold race horses, Bray and Brent cleaning the stalls and doing the daily chores. Both were great with horses. They took the job when they were fourteen and needed work in a place they could walk to. During football season, the Knolls had other hands, including Dallas who came in and helped. But seeing as Norton was a football fan, he tended to work alongside them. His wife and my momma were longtime friends, going back way before any of us came.

I parked the truck and left the keys in the ignition. No reason to take them out. No one was going to come down and steal it. We'd know before they left the city limits. Momma opened the front door and called, "You're home early. Dinner's on the stove. I got Women's Auxiliary at the church house tonight. Momma's busy, busy, busy."

I walked closer to the house before answering, "Dix and me are taking a picnic down to the lake this evening."

Momma winced and visibly shook. "I ain't looking to be a grand-mamma yet. You mind that."

"Dix ain't like that, Momma."

She scoffed. "It ain't Dixie Monroe that I'm worried about."

I grinned. "She's different. Trust me."

"Yes, she is, so keep it in your pants down at that lake."

Momma was never one to beat around the bush when discussing sex with us. She was honest and open about it. Becoming a widow by the time we were old enough to need "the talk" about sex probably had a lot to do with that. We didn't have a dad, so Momma made sure we were all well informed.

"I'd tell you to take a condom, but I want to believe you respect that girl enough not to be having sex with her out by her daddy's lake. You should fear Luke enough not to do that."

"I love her. Told you that. And yes, even if she asked me to, I wouldn't do it at the lake."

"Luke would shoot you and I'd die trying to save your stupid ass."

If God was ever going to leave a woman alone to raise five teenage boys, then he chose the right woman for the task. "No one will die, she'll remain a virgin, and we will enjoy her momma's meatloaf, just happy to be together."

Momma nodded and replied, "That's good. Now grab y'all some of that lemon pound cake I left on the counter. You need to contribute to the meal. Ain't the woman's job to always feed the man. Best you remember that."

I did as I was told, then changed into some clothes that didn't have that bleach water scent from the mopping I had to do at work, back in the meat department. Once I was ready, I paused by my dresser and opened the bottom drawer. I grabbed a condom because I'd lied. If Dixie asked me to make love to her tonight, I'd chance certain death at the end of a shotgun barrel, with her daddy yanking the trigger.

chapter
TWELVE

Dixie Monroe

I HADN'T ASKED to see the letters. I'd needed that moment to be about us. If that was the last time Asher Sutton would hold me, then I wanted nothing else. I wasn't sure I ever wanted to read them. I didn't know my mother. She hadn't been around long enough for me to remember her. Reading her words didn't mean a lot to me. There was someone else I wanted to talk to. Someone who could tell me the truth. And if he didn't know the truth, then we could find it together.

The man who'd raised and loved me was my father. Even if he wasn't my blood. He was my dad, nothing could change that. I just hoped he felt the same way, because I had to face this with him. I couldn't face it with Asher or Steel.

Daddy was out at the stable with his newest purchase, a pretty quarter horse that Mom had seen and wanted when they'd gone to the sale, initially to buy some cattle. Mom had married Daddy when I was little. She was a wonderful woman who made him happy. She loved me and we loved her. My family was perfect to me.

Having that ruined in any way wasn't easy. The one thing I always had to hold onto in my life and depend on felt like it was teetering on the brink of falling apart. Maybe another person wouldn't be so determined to know the truth no holding onto the love and security I had would be simpler, but I needed to face the past. I had to ask daddy why he'd loved me anyway, raised me as his own, how he could even stand to look at me when I was a constant reminder of his wife's betrayal.

As a kid, whenever I thought there was a monster under my bed, I would grab a baseball bat and immediately search for it, instead of hiding under the covers. I never backed down and hid. I faced my fears. This was no different. It was the biggest fear I'd ever faced but I was ready.

"Hey, buttercup," Daddy called, stepping from the stables. He'd seen me headed his way.

"Hey," I replied, my voice cracking, tears quickly filling my eyes. Apparently, this wasn't like fighting the monsters under my bed. This was scarier. I loved this man, trusted him with my life. I knew he'd be there no matter what. But I knew my questions would hurt him.

His smile sagged. "Who the hell do I need to beat up? Why're there tears in my girl's eyes?" He took three long strides, grabbed both my arms, and looked down at me with sad eyes. "Is this another Sutton boy's doing? Cause if it is, I'm gonna go burn that place down. I swear to God, I'm sick of those boys hurting you. What else have they done?"

The fact that he didn't know the truth was even more apparent as he spoke. I had to tell him. I was going to destroy the love this man always had for me. Could I do that? I felt my knees go weak. I couldn't lose my daddy.

"Alright, buttercup, you're scaring me. Is your momma okay?" he asked, glancing back at the house.

I nodded. "It's not about her," I managed to say without sobbing.

"Talk, darling, I can't fix this if I don't know what I need to fix."

My daddy always tried to fix my problems. But he hadn't been able to mend my broken heart when Asher had turned away from me. And now, he would not be able to fix what I had to tell him, either. The problem was standing right before him. I was the unfixable mistake.

"I heard Asher Sutton was home. Is this about him?" Daddy asked, his voice laced with anger. "He's a man now and I don't have a problem beating the hell outta him."

"Daddy," I said, interrupting his angry tirade about Asher. "Did you know . . . did you . . . I . . . ." How did I ask my father whether he knew his wife was unfaithful? I couldn't do this. Could I do this? God, this was too much.

"Did I know what, baby? What's bothering you?" he replied. His words were gentler as he pulled me closer to his chest like he was protecting me. And he didn't even know from what.

"My . . . mother . . . did she . . ." I stopped, swallowed hard, because I felt sick. Hearing this was one thing, but repeating it was another thing altogether.

"You said this wasn't about Mom," he whispered with concern, gazing again at the house. He didn't understand.

I shook my head. "No, the woman . . . my real mother," I replied, his body immediately tensing. We never talked about her, ever, not once. I didn't know why she had left. Had she left because of an affair? Did he not know that I was the product of that affair?

"Has someone contacted you?" he asked, his voice strained and quavering.

I shook my head. I'd once planned on finding her. Now, I never wanted to see her. She'd ruined my life, leaving lies behind that destroyed everything. "Did you know she had an affair with Vance Sutton?" I asked before I could stop myself. Closing my eyes tightly, I immediately wanted to take those words back. I did not want him to know this. I loved him. He was my daddy. I couldn't lose that. Ever.

"Honey, mentally, she wasn't well. But yes, I knew. How did you find out about this?" His words surprised me. I hadn't expected him to know that much, if anything. "Do the Sutton boys know?"

I nodded. "Yes, Asher found letters that Millie wrote to Vance. They said some things . . ." tears were now spilling free down my face. I couldn't hold it in any longer. I'd faced this fear and now I had to wait, see what happened next.

Daddy stared down at me frowning with worry on his face and then slowly understanding lit his eyes. He closed them tightly, muttering a curse, before pulling me against him and squeezing. "Oh, no, baby, I know what Asher must have read. It's not what you think, buttercup. You're my princess. You hear me? You're mine. I got proof of that. Those letters were from a mentally unstable woman. A woman who hurt others as if life was a game. Millie's beauty was something she used as a weapon against people."

I pulled away from him to search his face. "I'm not Vance Sutton's daughter?" I repeated it, said it again, making sure I wasn't hearing him wrong.

"No!" Daddy yelled angrily. "Hell no! You're all mine! Although Millie tried to destroy me and Vance Sutton with her lie. I had a paternity test done when you were born because Vance demanded it. He wanted proof you weren't his. But understand this, from the moment they handed you to me, minutes after you were born, you became mine, right then and there. You stole my heart, a heart I didn't think could heal, but you healed it the moment I looked into your eyes and no piece of paper could have taken that away from me. I wouldn't have cared what that paper said, you were my baby girl. I was willing to fight for you. I wanted you. Yes, Millie had broken me, but you, Dixie Monroe, you saved me from the darkness. You were my miracle. You lit my life."

I let my Daddy hold me and cried.

Three Years Ago . . .

MY BIGGEST FEAR was that, one day, Asher would grow to resent me. Years from now, when we were married with children, when I had to drive them to ballet, football practice or soccer, and sex was something we'd have to find time for, when the washing machine was broken, and the car needed new brakes, that Asher's decision not to play football for Florida and have a chance to go pro one day would haunt him for the rest of his life. That being a husband and dad wouldn't be enough for him. That he would wonder every day what his life could have been like and I would be the one he'd blame for taking his dream away from him. I'd only dreamed of one thing in my life and that was to have Asher Sutton's love. I had that. My dream had come true. I was living it, but Asher was giving up his, for me, and that was scaring me. As much as I begged him not to withdraw from Florida, he swore he couldn't be happy without me close and in his life.

Momma said that it was his choice and I had to stop worrying about it. But I did. It kept me up at night. Asher was the reason the football team won state two years in a row. They even talked about him on the news—where he'd sign, whether he'd lead an undefeated college football team, just like he'd done in high school. He was important. And I would be the girl who kept him from achieving all this.

Selfishly, I wanted him close. I couldn't imagine not seeing him daily. Distance wouldn't make me love him less. I'd loved him since I was thirteen and that wasn't going to change. We'd stopped going to Jack's and now we did things without his brothers and friends. We went to the lake or sat out on the football field at night, instead, talking about high school. *How it was almost over for him and how my time here seemed endless. Some nights he'd take me to dinner and a movie, normally on the days he got his paycheck. He gave half to his momma to pay the bills, all the boys did and the other half he spent on us. That made me feel guilty because I wanted to help out, but Asher never let me.*

When his old blue truck pulled into the drive and his brothers weren't in the back, I knew tonight we'd be discussing this again. We'd talked about it repeatedly, but now that his final decision needed be made next week, I had one last chance to convince him to go to Florida and play football.

The days were warmer now, but the nights were still cool, the heat of summer still two months off. My arms were bare, so I pulled the white sweater I was carrying over my shoulders and went out to his truck. He was grinning. "I got paid early. Want to see a movie?"

What I wanted was for him to save his money. "I'd rather do something where we can talk."

He frowned. "That sounds like something serious."

It was, so I replied, "I want to spend time with you. No movie. Just us. Alone."

He gave me a crooked grin. "Okay. I can live with that. Then tell me what you'd like to do."

"Can we ride out to Hillview Peak?" I asked.

Asher's eyebrows shot up and I knew why. That was where people went to park. It was known for its dark, secluded location. On any given night, you could find sweaty couples having sex in cramped back seats. No one ever talked about it, but everyone knew what happened on Hillview Peak.

I watched as a million different thoughts flashed through his expressive eyes. "Dix, uh, baby, if you're ready for that . . . I mean, if you want it . . . trust me, I want the very same thing. But I'm not having your first time be at Hillview Peak. Give me some notice and I can come up with a better place than my truck."

His truck. He'd lost his virginity in his truck. There'd been a lot of girls in there. Now, there was just me. I knew that. I trusted him completely. I was ready and although I'd always imagined losing my virginity in Asher Sutton's truck, I didn't really want it to happen there. I wanted "us" to be different. I didn't hold all the girls he'd been with, the ones that came before me, against him, because I wasn't jealous. I just didn't want our first time to be the same, or even similar, to anyone else he'd been with in the past.

I'd intended to talk him into going to Florida and now we were somehow talking about sex. This wasn't exactly how I meant for it to happen. I wanted to convince him to live his dream. We could still be together, though it would be hard on both of us. Part of me, a part I wasn't very proud of, thought that sex would bind him to me, keep him from going off and realizing that I wasn't the one for him. Then there was that other small voice in my head that said I wanted him to be my first and there was no reason to keep waiting. But the biggest part of me wanted Asher inside of me, to have that kind of connection with him.

"I just wanted to talk at Hillview. It seemed secluded and the stars there are beautiful."

"When have you seen the stars at Hillview Peak?" he asked with a scowl that made me laugh.

"I snuck up there with Scarlet when we were thirteen to see if we could spy anyone having sex . . . mostly it was curiosity."

Asher seemed relieved. "What? Scarlet wasn't having sex at thirteen?"

"Not yet," I replied, laughing. There was no reason to defend my best friend. She'd been boy crazy since ten. And it was exactly one month after she turned fourteen that she happily lost her virginity.

"I don't want anyone seeing us going there. They'll talk," Asher said.

"You've been there many times. It won't be a big deal."

He reached down and laced his fingers through mine. "You're a big deal. My big deal. And I don't want anyone thinking I'm screwing you in my damn pickup truck. Especially at Hillview Peak."

Asher rarely cursed around me. The fact he did it now only made his words sweeter. He was protecting me. Asher cherished what he had. All the things my momma said I was supposed to expect from a guy and should never settle for any less. Asher would always be more. More than any guy could ever be.

chapter
THIRTEEN

Asher Sutton

"YOU BETTER EAT them biscuits. I didn't get up and fix them for you to just look at them," Momma said, as she stared at my plate and the food I'd barely touched. My appetite was gone. Vanished.

"Yes, Momma," I replied before I forced a bite into my mouth and chewed.

Steel had hurried up, finished his breakfast, then left. Didn't even look me in the eye, not once. That was good. He needed to keep his distance until I was able to calm down.

"Can I have another?" Dallas asked like a damn five-year-old.

"Go get it yourself! She's not your waitress!" I snapped at him angrily.

His eyes got big as he stood up with his plate and headed to the stove.

"Okay, what's got you all tied up in knots? You weren't here this morning and Bray was out looking for you while the rest of them tried to distract me. I raised every one of you. I know when you don't come home at night and I know when Dallas is trying to charm me so that someone else can get away with something."

Dallas smirked as he sat down with another plate of biscuits smothered in tomato gravy. "Figures," he laughed.

I refused to tell Momma what was wrong. There was no reason for her to suffer that kind of pain right now. She had good memories of my dad and it needed to stay that way. Telling her wouldn't make it any better. Hurting her for no reason was unnecessary.

"I'm adjusting to being home again. Steel broke it off with Dixie and I'm not gonna lie, I'm glad. Dixie needs to move on and not with one of my brothers."

I hoped my voice didn't betray me. Damn, it sounded like it did.

Momma cocked an eyebrow and sat down across from me with a cup of coffee in her hand. "I call BS," she just said. She sipped her coffee and studied me. "BS, you hear me. I don't buy it," making her point now more aggressively.

"Momma, let's just leave him alone," Bray said. He was the only one brave enough to say something like that to Momma. Except for me, and I wasn't speaking.

Momma turned to glare down the table at Bray who was now looking like a little boy with his hand in the cookie jar. I would've laughed, if I wasn't so fucked up. Dallas and Brent both snickered. They knew what was coming next.

"I don't recall asking you what to do. I carried him for nine months and through ten hours of labor. Then I cleaned his nasty butt, nursed him when he was sick, held his hand while he got stitches, and let him puke all over me whenever he got food poisoning. So do *not* tell me what I can and can't do. *If* and *when* I want to know about one of my boys, I will ask and get an answer. And you might be next, so shut your mouth and eat your breakfast.

You're in *my* house."

Bray dropped his head and replied meekly, "Yes, ma'am."

Momma swung her attention back to me. "Now, last time I checked, you kicked that sweet Dixie Monroe to the curb, without even a backwards glance. Wouldn't say a word or look at her. I was worried about you getting too serious. You were young, so I didn't push it. But three years have passed and when you should be attached to some girl you've met at college by now, you're back here still looking heartbroken. Ain't right. Don't make sense to me. When a man looks like you, he has women beating down his door. But you're alone. Explain that to me! It has to be you pushing them away. Steel loves that girl. He's bought her a ring God knows he can't afford, and now he's broken up with her two days after you get home. I smell shit. S.H.I.T."

I glanced down the table at Bray, but he was eating and not looking our way. Momma had put him in his place. Brent was watching us with worry in his eyes. He knew I couldn't tell Momma the truth. They all did, but not one of them was trying to help me out. Suddenly, they were all mute.

"Maybe, he didn't love her enough. Enough to fight for her and make sure she was protected from everything that could hurt her. Maybe, he wouldn't sacrifice his happiness for hers. Maybe . . ." I stopped and stood up. "Momma, I love you, but I can't talk about this. Not right now," I said, leaving my plate on the table and heading for the door. If Steel could run out, so could I. Facing Momma right now wasn't the best idea.

"You found them letters . . . now, didn't you?" Momma's words stopped me as my hand touched the screen. I froze. The letters. If she knew about the letters, then she knew . . .

What the fuck?

Turning around, I looked at her and saw the sadness in her eyes. "What letters?" I needed her to spell it out. If she was referring to the letters I found, then she shouldn't have allowed Steel or me anywhere near Dixie Monroe in the first place.

"The letters from that woman to your daddy. I didn't know where he hid them. But three years ago, you found them, didn't you?" She nodded as if I'd confirmed this. "I wondered once back then when you looked so miserable, but then I thought, no, surely not. If you found something like that, you'd ask me about it, but you never did, so I figured it was something else. Now I see I made a *grave* mistake."

I stared at my mother. She knew. But she . . ."Why would you let us, let *me* be with Dixie that way if you knew?" I was trying to grasp the fact that my mother knowingly had allowed Steel and myself to commit incest. The fucking world that I knew was warping before me.

Momma stood up and shook her head. "I'd have never let such a thing happen. That girl ain't your daddy's child. Luke Monroe has a paternity test that proves Dixie is his. Millie Monroe was the most beautiful woman in the county and probably the state, too. She could seduce a man like nothing I'd ever seen, but that woman, she was insane. Mentally screwed up, I tell you. She set her sight on your daddy and that meant she eventually got him. Your daddy was a man, that's the only excuse I got for him back then and now. I forgave him a long time ago. Understand this, he never stopped trying to make it up to me. He did love me, he just let temptation get the best of him. Not the first and definitely not the last man to do that."

If my daddy were still alive, I'd go kill him right now. Listening to my momma talk about him being seduced by another woman pissed the hell out of me.

"When I was gone to the doctor one day, Millie came to the barn and, well . . . she did some things any man would have a hard time refusing. Your daddy made a mistake. Then," she sighed and added, "Millie came back and did it again a few more times after that. Your daddy was weak, so when Millie got pregnant, we didn't know if it could be your daddy's child. He admitted it to me right then. Everything he'd done. I was pregnant with Steel at the time. I had three babies I was taking care of and money was tight, you see. Your daddy used Millie as an escape from the troubles we were going through. I thought I'd leave him for a while, but he was so pitiful, and I loved him very much. It took a couple of years, but I finally forgave him. Anyway, when that little girl was born, I wanted a paternity test. So did your daddy. If that baby was his, we needed to know, but it wasn't. Dixie was Luke's. Period."

"Holy fuck," Bray swore, reminding me we weren't alone, my brothers were still sitting there and listening to every word.

"Can't believe I was even born. You shoulda killed him," Dallas muttered.

Momma turned around and faced them all. "I loved that man. He loved and adored all of you. He was a good man who had weak moments. He made a mistake and I forgave him. It don't change the fact you were his whole world. He loved each of you." Her tone was determined and it showed she meant what she was saying. I wasn't sure I could ever forgive the man, but he was gone and being mad at him was pointless. In the end, he'd left us all anyway.

Momma looked back to me. "Where were those letters?" she asked.

"Loose floorboard in the attic," I told her.

She nodded. "I should have checked that place out before I let you move up there. I knew you were sweet on that girl. She looks just like her momma, but she ain't a thing like her. She's got her daddy's heart and Luke Monroe is as good a man as you'll find. He tried to make it work with Millie, even when he knew she was crazy. Millie ran off and left him with that little girl, and it was the best thing that could've happened, both for Dixie and Luke. She didn't need that woman in her life. She turned out to be a fine young woman. The day I heard Millie had dropped dead out in California, I didn't even feel pity. I felt nothing but some relief that she'd never try and come back into Dixie's life. Dixie is a beautiful woman inside and out." Momma paused, then reached over and squeezed my arm. "A woman your brother loved enough to propose to. Remember that, okay, Asher?"

Remember that. There was no forgetting.

Three Years Ago . . .

I COULDN'T SLEEP. Dixie's face and the sounds she made while I'd been inside her the first time replayed over and over in my mind. It was a memory that would never grow old. I also wanted to do it again and again until neither of us could walk. I thought being with Dixie couldn't get any better. I'd been wrong. The sex was life-changing. Feeling her naked against me, her thighs open, their insides pressed against my hips had felt like heaven on earth. Nothing that felt that good could ever be wrong.

I'd had sex with eight other girls in the past, all of them older than me and with tricks that I hadn't known until they taught me. I appreciated those lessons. I enjoyed every one of them. I was a guy, so I won't deny it. That sex was amazing. But none of those experiences had prepared me for how it would feel sliding inside Dixie for the first time, knowing I loved her. I didn't want to hurt her, I wanted it to be a memory she could cherish forever. I'd been about to explode inside her when her nails dug into my back and she cried my name with a scream. Dixie's head was thrown back, her body trembling with release, and I could feel her pleasure churning through her body like a twister. I knew from Bray's stories that virgins didn't orgasm the very first time, and even though I'd wanted that for Dixie, I didn't expect it. I just wanted her to enjoy it.

While standing in the middle of my bedroom, I decided to move the furniture. I wanted to bring Dixie up here one evening, maybe next week when Momma was at church and my brothers were all gone. I wanted to be with her, here in my room. The squeaky floor under the bed would be an issue if we ever did it late at night when everyone was here and asleep. I wanted to be with her in a bed and not in the grass for once. She didn't seem to mind the blanket on the grass by the lake nor did she mind my truck. But she deserved more than that.

It had been three weeks since we made love the first time, but we'd managed to do it as often as we could since then. Dixie was sore the first few times and I'd been taking it easy with her. But the more we did it, the wilder she was getting. The memory of her begging me last night was giving me a boner. I had those a lot lately just thinking of Dixie.

The shower would ease me some, but that was always just a short-lived release. I couldn't seem to get her off my mind even after thrusting my cock into my hand in the shower. I was going to need to wear myself out. I could move furniture, then clean. My room needed it, especially if I was going to bring Dixie up here and make love to her in my bed.

I moved the bed away from the wall. Then I stepped into the space to make sure the headboard didn't break because I'd yanked it sideways from the wallboard. The floor beneath my left foot moved and made a soft clunking sound. That had to be the source of the squeak. I looked down at the loose board now catty-cornered under my foot. I hadn't noticed it when I first moved up here. But then I'd had my bed sitting over this spot all along.

I squatted, grabbed the board to see if it could be nailed down, but my eyes found something else. Something that had been hidden there for a very long time. I didn't know that yet, but I was curious. I picked the old shoe box up, anxious to open it, the idea of it being a family heirloom exciting me to no end.

I sat on the edge of my bed and slowly opened the box. Several letters were inside, folded neatly one on top of the other. I lifted one from the pile and wondered if I should open it, if I had any right to do it. If they contained secrets, maybe those secrets were meant to stay hidden for a reason.

My curiosity got the best of me. I carefully unfolded the pages. The words were handwritten and as I read them slowly, my world as I knew it began to change. Darkness engulfed me and any joy, any happiness I felt was ripped from me one word at a time. I wanted to stop reading and burn the whole box, watch it catch fire and pretend I ever read any of it . . . but I knew I couldn't. Every single word was seared into my brain forever. I read every letter, every page. I knew I had to break the heart of the only girl I'd ever love, even if that love was all wrong.

chapter
FOURTEEN

Dixie Monroe

SCARLET'S WHITE CAMARO came down my long driveway. I sat in the porch swing watching as she made her way to the house. We hadn't talked much in the past two days. She seemed to understand that I needed some distance with Asher being back.

She had no idea how crazy things had gotten.

When she stopped and her door swung open, I realized that Scarlet might be my best friend, but there were things I just wasn't ready to talk with her about. I wasn't telling anyone about this until I got myself mentally prepared to tell Asher that we weren't related. Once I realized that my daddy was my daddy and that he loved me even more than I'd known, I was left knowing that this horrible secret that made Asher leave me three years ago no longer stood between us.

Running to him had been the first thing I wanted to do, but then I remembered Steel. I had to deal with Steel first and see where we stood. I had to think about this, think it all over and decide on the right thing to do, so I sat on my porch and listened to my mom humming as she cooked lunch, knowing that I was safe. My life wasn't about to be pulled from under me. So I had to give myself time to be able to make the right decision.

Scarlet spoke as she approached, "Since my best friend couldn't pick up a phone and call me, or heck even text me, I figured I better check on her. The Suttons got you in a tangled web?" She walked up the steps onto the front porch that wrapped around our house. I replied, "Sorry. I'm spending a bit of time with my thoughts," before patting the empty spot on the swing beside me. "Sit and talk if you'd like."

Scarlet flicked her red hair behind her shoulder, smirking and shooting back, "Fine, but only 'cause you're sexy," she teased, before sitting next to me. She gave the swing a big push with her legs, then tucked her knees beneath her chin. "Brent said there's been some drama."

I confirmed, "Yep, you could say that. But right now I want to stay away from it. Try peace for a day or two. I have to talk to Steel, but not just yet."

Scarlet sighed. "Please don't tell me you're gonna break it off with him. He loves you. Don't mess it up because of Asher's sexy ass. He ain't worth it, Dixie."

She didn't know any of it. But hearing her talk about Asher like he wasn't worth the fight was hard. Because he was. Well worth it all. Steel did love me and I had to figure out if what I felt for him was love. I knew I was in love with Asher. I adored him. He was everything I wanted. But he was also dangerous, could hurt me so easily, and now he might not want me at all. Steel did. At least I thought he did before he found out about the letters. Now he and Asher would have to know the truth.

"You talked to Brent today?" I asked wanting to change the subject.

"Yeah," she replied, then looked out at the yard. "I also talked to Bray."

If she'd talked to Bray, that wasn't a big deal . . . or it wouldn't have been if she hadn't said it like she felt guilty about something. I studied her face for a moment and wondered if I'd been so wrapped up in my own life that I'd missed something important happening in hers.

"Why did you talk to Bray?" I asked, trying to sound casual.

She didn't look at me, but the way her shoulders tensed wasn't good, not good at all. "Scarlet," I said, "look at me."

"Do you ever wonder what Bray's thinking? He's so guarded. He rarely smiles." She paused and a small smile touched her lips. "But when he does smile, it's really something."

Whoa. This was not good.

"Scarlet, um, is there something you need to tell me?"

She released a long sigh, then turned her head toward me and rested her cheek on her knees. "Probably shouldn't. It's bad. I'm bad for even thinking it. What kind of person does that? He's Brent's twin brother, but they're so different. Bray's moody and mysterious and he's got this sexy, angry look about him that makes me feel funny in my stomach. Do you get what I'm saying?"

The Sutton boys were trouble. Beautiful trouble. Lots of stinking trouble. And Bray was the worst of them all.

"Bray isn't like Brent and that's a good thing. Brent loves you, while Bray likes all girls, and he especially likes getting blowjobs from them. You've heard the stories on how he gets off. Having girls drop to their knees before he gets rough with them. Remember what Jenn said about Bray? How he gagged her and called her names, while he held the back of her head?"

Scarlet grinned and pressed her lips together. "Yeah, but she also said it was sexy and then she went back for more."

What? "Scar, please tell me you're kidding," I replied. Nothing about that sounded sexy.

Scarlet lifted a shoulder and gave a little shrug. "The idea of Bray talking dirty to me while getting off . . . well, it kind of excites me." She then squeezed her eyes tightly together. "That makes me a slut, doesn't it? I sound awful just saying that."

I had no answer. No right response to give her. I didn't think that sounded exciting at all. The rumors about Bray and his sex-capades were rampant, not just in Malroy, but throughout the entire county. Girls loved him, but they said he wasn't sweet and easy. Bray took what he wanted, when he wanted it, and how he wanted it.

"If Asher," she said, lowering her voice, "pushed you down to your knees in front of him and shoved his dick down your throat, telling you that you had a dirty little mouth and called you his bad, naughty girl, saying that you needed to be punished, maybe even spanked, you . . . that wouldn't turn you on?"

I couldn't respond. The idea of being on my knees in front of Asher and being able to bring him pleasure made my heart race and my body feel feverish. Okay, maybe she had a point.

"But you love Brent. Why would the idea of Bray doing these things excite you?"

She turned her gaze back toward the yard. She wouldn't look at me. What wasn't she telling me? Had I completely missed something important happening in her life? "He's different. I like it when I can make him smile. He doesn't smile enough."

We were two peas in a pod. Both torn between two Sutton boys. Maybe our reasons were different, but who was I to judge? I wrapped my arm around Scarlet's shoulders and rested my head against hers. With a shove of my feet, I got us swinging again, then pulled my feet up under me. "Bray can't be trusted with your heart. You know that, right?" I reminded her.

She didn't reply right away. We listened to Mom humming

and the sound of the tractor way out in the field. It was peaceful. Until Scarlet replied, "Just like Asher can't be trusted with yours."

She was right, but I hated hearing that. The front door then opened, Mom sticking her head through it and twisting her face toward us to speak, "I have peach cobbler hot from the oven and vanilla ice cream for the top. Y'all want me to bring two bowls?" She then came out the rest of the way and waited for our response. Seeing her smiling blond head, slightly wide hips, and makeup-free face beaming at me with such love and adoration made me want to get up and hold her for hours just because she was there. She wasn't what the world would consider beautiful, but to me, she was the most beautiful woman in the world. Especially where it counted the most. She'd loved a little girl who wasn't hers and made all her bad dreams go away. She'd been there the day I got my period and got scared out of my mind, and she'd held me when Asher left me. I was the luckiest girl in the world to have her as my mom. She was the kind of woman I hoped to be one day.

"We'll come inside and eat some with you," I told her before standing up.

"I need some cobbler," Scarlet agreed.

I walked over to my mom, wrapped my arms around her and said, "I love you," swallowing the emotion in my throat, and pushing back the tears what were threatening to come.

She gave me a quick squeeze, kissed my cheek and replied, "I love you more, princess. Never forget that." That had always been her response whenever I told her I loved her.

Asher Sutton

I HADN'T SEEN or spoken to Steel in two days. I knew Bray had told him everything that Momma told us. He let me know that Steel knew the truth about Dixie and the letters, and once I got my emotions under control, I had planned on going to Dixie and telling her everything. It was the only thing I'd been able to think about. But then I realized it wasn't my place to tell her. Steel had proposed to Dixie. Momma had been sure to remind me of that.

I waited for something to happen, but Steel never came to find me. I was getting tired of waiting on him to do something.

He'd left early this morning to go mend the south fence. Bray said it was Steel's turn to pull wire when I asked where he was during breakfast. I had to talk to Steel because I wanted to go to Dixie, but I couldn't. I wasn't free to do that. The idea that I could hold her, that I could love her freely again was taunting me. The way I felt about her wasn't wrong or messed up, it was allowed. I was allowed to worship Dixie, to tell her that she owned my soul, that she was everything to me.

But I was waiting on my own little brother to do . . . something . . . anything.

When I got down to the barn, I could see the farm truck headed toward me, knowing Steel was in it. The posts and wire he hadn't needed were clanking around in the bed, the diesel engine rumbling to an idle, then to a stop behind the barn. Steel climbed from the truck and slammed the door without looking at me. The anger on his face wasn't what I'd been expecting to find. I hadn't done anything to piss him off. He was the one who'd hurt Dixie.

"What?" I asked, forcing him to look at me and meeting his glare.

He let out a hard laugh. "What," he repeated, "I'm waiting on you to tell me you're going to see Dixie today. That's why you're here, isn't it? To tell me you're going to talk to her. To warn me you're about to swoop in and give her what she wants. What she's wanted all her life." He pulled off his work gloves and threw them down on the ground. "What the fuck do I do with that? I can't compete. So go get her, Asher. Go fucking take her away from me." He then spun and stalked toward the barn.

Steel loved her, maybe not the way I did, but he loved her all the same. And I loved him, he was my little brother and I'd always been there whenever he needed me. I'd taught him how to throw a football. Where to hit a baseball on the barrel of your bat. How to tackle with your head across.

I loved Dixie. But my lost chance with her. Steel was there for her when she needed someone to comfort her after I'd walked away from her without a word. I didn't deserve her. Steel was the better man. Deep in my heart, I knew that as I called his name and he stopped. He turned just before entering the barn. The anger in his eyes was now gone, replaced by the kind of pain that further cemented my decision.

"What," he replied, "what, Asher?"

"Go get her! She was yours until now. She hasn't been mine in a long time. I've lived three years believing what I had with her was wrong and disgusting. You only lived that hell for a day. Your love for her is still pure. It's you she needs right now, not me. I'm pretty sure I'm broken beyond repair and won't ever be whole again."

The tension in Steel's shoulders loosened, his eyes then becoming those of a worried brother. "You're not broken. You're a good man, Asher. A great one if you ask me."

He was wrong, but he loved me. His love was special, exactly the kind of love I wanted for Dixie. She wouldn't ever be faced with the dark demons that had taken over my life, demons I wasn't sure would ever go away. Finding out the truth didn't magically fix me. It freed me, but it didn't fix me. That required something I wasn't willing to take—Dixie's love. I couldn't have it. It would never be mine again.

"Thanks," I told him, "but I'll be leaving next month. She needs a man who'll be here for her. One who will show her the sunshine every damn day. I have too much darkness in my soul to give Dixie the light she deserves."

Steel stood there staring at me. Finally, he nodded in agreement. "Okay," he replied. "I do love her, you know."

"I know," I quietly assured him.

He wiped his hands on his jeans, then flashed a small smile, before jogging down to his truck. Watching him go wasn't easy, but it was the right thing to do.

The barn door opened and I glanced back to see Dallas standing there wearing nothing but a pair of white shorts and a set of boxing gloves. I hadn't known anyone was inside the barn. Dallas was just staring at me.

"I love all my brothers, but just to clarify, Asher, you're the best one of them. We all know it. Even Steel." Dallas spoke, giving me a sad smile. He then lifted his chin toward the inside of the barn. "Come on in and beat the shit out of that heavy bag. I just finished and I'm about to lift weights. The bag is all yours if you want it."

Hitting something sounded really fucking good. I walked up to the barn as Dallas pulled his gloves off and slapped me in the stomach with them. "Here you go, old man," he teased.

I grabbed the gloves and felt a genuine grin tug at my lips for the first time in a really long while. "This old man could beat your ass."

Dallas chuckled and pointed at himself, before flexing his impressive arms. "Dude, you looked at me lately? I'm a beast," he replied. "A monster."

In return I laughed, really laughed, all the muscles one used to do that finally coming to life again. They'd lain unused for years.

"Yes, you are, little brother. Both a beast and a monster," I said. The surprised expression on Dallas's face was quickly replaced by a big grin of his own.

Steel Sutton

WHILE PULLING ONTO the dirt road that connected our driveway with Dixie's, I noticed Bray's truck parked in the field. Slowing down, I checked to see if he needed anything. But when I saw a red head and a pair of tits rising and falling like the sea, I shook my head grinning and kept driving toward Dixie's house. In broad daylight, the bastard had a girl out there, fucking away without a care. Dude was crazy. My brother was nuts.

Dixie and me hadn't had sex. We'd been together now for eleven months. It was my longest stint of celibacy since I was fifteen and Brenda Vickers first showed me her eighteen-year-old tits, then how good it felt to slide my dick into a hot, wet pussy. Sex became as important as oxygen to me. But then I'd fallen in love with Dixie and waiting on her becoming even more important. Turning down willing women wasn't easy sometimes, but Dixie was worth the wait. She was better than a meaningless night with some easy lay. Dixie was worth it all.

Seeing Bray getting some made me a little jealous. I was tired of masturbating. But what he had was cheap and would be over soon. I had something more with Dixie, something worth the sacrifice, and the long wait that went along with it.

I breathed a sigh of relief when I saw Dixie's Jeep parked outside, so I hurried to her door. I didn't want to wait any longer. For two days, Dixie hadn't called or texted me. I was so damn sure that Asher would come and take her away from me anyway, so I didn't try to contact her either. I believed Dixie loved me. She'd told me she loved me, but then again, I wasn't sure she loved me as much as Asher. Their history was longer than ours, longer and more complicated. I always felt like second fiddle to him. But now that he wasn't planning on coming for her, she would be mine again.

The front door opened and Dixie stepped outside wearing a pair of cutoff jeans and a plaid shirt that was tied in a knot, her stomach visible for an inch or two. My heart began beating rapidly. She was barefoot and looked exactly like every southern boy's fantasy. Any boy's fantasy. "Hey," she said with the tiniest of smiles. She didn't look like she was hurting. None of the pain I'd seen in her eyes two days back was there anymore. I wasn't sure how I felt about that. I didn't want her hurting, but I also hoped she loved me enough to hurt from our break-up.

"How are you?" I asked, searching her face.

She shrugged. "Good. Better. I talked to my daddy."

The way she said "my daddy" with relief in her voice told me her father had cleared the air of the lies that we all had believed.

"So you know the truth, then?" I asked.

She frowned. Blew through her lips. "Yeah, but it isn't what Asher thinks."

I nodded. "We know. Momma told us."

Dixie's eyes went wide and she glanced toward our house. "Oh, really, when?"

"Two mornings ago. I would've been here sooner, but we all kinda needed some time . . . to deal . . . you know?"

She turned her eyes back to me. The sudden sadness in them made me want to kick myself. Why did I tell her I'd known for two days without coming to her? How stupid was that of me?

"I'm sorry," I muttered, "so sorry."

She forced a smile and shook her head. "No, it's okay. I also knew and didn't come to you. I just . . ." she paused and nervously swallowed. "Never mind. I'm not making sense. It's been a crazy few days, I guess."

"Yeah, it has," I agreed. I then reached out to take her hand in mine. "But I never stopped loving you. I loved you even when I thought it was wrong. I couldn't turn that off."

She drew inward, tensed, her gaze flicking back toward my house again. I knew then that this was about Asher. She was waiting on him, which was what I should've expected. I should've known this would happen. He was the one she'd lost and never gotten over. It was written all over her face.

"I waited on him," I told her. "He's the reason I didn't come until now. I was giving him a chance to come to you. But he came to me this morning and told me to come see you. Not to make you wait. That I loved you more than he ever could and you deserved that. Not him."

The pain in her eyes intensified and I wanted to roar at the unfairness. Why did Dixie have to do this to me? I'd waited on her, been faithful to her because I loved her and wanted it to work. Why did she have to want him more? He'd sent me. He'd let her go.

I was here. He wasn't.

"Oh," she said, unable to look up. She studied her hands instead.

Just a fucking "oh."

"Dixie, do you still want this? Us?" I asked, willing her to at least look at me. To give me something, any damn thing.

Finally, she raised her gaze and asked, "Steel, do *you* want this?"

Did she even have to ask? "More than anything, Dixie."

She didn't respond right away. Instead, she waited a few moments, before releasing the softest of sighs. "Okay, yes, I want this, too."

Relief washed over me. I wanted to pound my chest. I'd won. Dixie was mine. Dixie Monroe was the most gorgeous woman I'd ever laid eyes on and she'd chosen me over my brother.

"I'll make you happy, Dixie. Baby, I swear."

She nodded, took a step toward me, laying her head on my chest. This was what I'd needed. What I wanted more than anything else. I could do without sex until she was ready. Just knowing that one day Dixie Monroe would share my bed made everything better. For now.

chapter SIXTEEN

Dixie Monroe

THE FOLLOWING WEEK, I saw Steel every day. But I never saw Asher. Not once. His truck was parked outside by the pump house, but when I came by, he never came around. I didn't ask and Steel didn't mention it. I felt like Steel was waiting on me to ask, and if I did, I would've failed some test of sorts.

Scarlet said to let go of the past, but I didn't know how to do that. Asher was more than just my past. He was a part of me. He owned a piece of my heart, possibly the biggest one of them all. You couldn't just ignore that because people told you to do so. Even if he didn't fight for us to be together, my heart didn't care, and the pain I felt from knowing that was unbearable still.

He still had the power to make me drop everything and go running to him with a crook of his finger. He still had that much hold over me. Though, it felt as if he were gone again. Scarlet said she'd seen him two days ago working in the barn with Bray doing some renovations. He was laughing and seemed less preoccupied than he'd been in the past three years. I was glad he wasn't living with the darkness that had eaten at him for so long. But I missed him. I wanted to see him like this. See the old Asher again.

"Damn, he's at it again," Steel muttered, drawing me from my thoughts. I turned to look what he was frowning at. I saw the back of Brent's head and the familiar red curls belonging to my best friend in the back of Bray's truck. I shook my head. Did they think parking out there was an actual hiding place?

"I swear, Bray can't get a full day of work in without getting him some."

I began to tell Steel it wasn't Bray, that it was Brent, but I stopped and looked again, squinting over the field. The sun and distance made it hard to see. That was definitely Scarlet's red hair. I would have known it anywhere. And that had to be Brent. She was attracted to Bray, but she wouldn't . . . actually sleep with him. She wouldn't. Would she?

"You want burgers for lunch or seafood? I'm good with either, starved through the gut," Steel said, snapping my gaze from Bray's truck. He didn't seem to notice that was Scarlet and until I knew what was going on, I wouldn't point that out to him.

"Uh . . . seafood is good," I replied.

I pulled my phone from my pocket and sent Scarlet a hopeful text: Please tell me that was Brent? She'd know what I meant.

"Another reason I love you. We think alike. Let's go," Steel said, turning and laughing. I smiled back at him, but the words wouldn't come. Telling Steel I loved him seemed wrong, especially now. I wasn't sure if I loved him like he loved me. Steel was good to me. Would've fought for me. I had to keep reminding myself of that daily.

I listened to Steel talk about the barn and all the renovations they were going to do. I didn't even wince when he said Asher's name, complaining that Asher was getting a job this summer working for Denver Watson, at the local Feed and Seed. He didn't understand why Asher couldn't help them work the family farm. I wanted to tell him that Asher knew they needed more money and the only way to get that was to work for someone else.

Instead, I asked, "What does your momma think?"

He rolled his eyes. "Momma thinks Asher hung the moon. You know that. She's so glad he's home for the summer, she'll agree with whatever he does."

"Or maybe she knows that Asher could make more to help pay the bills by working for someone else." Arguing with Steel was one thing. Defending Asher was another entirely. I knew it and I did it anyway. It was as if I couldn't control my mouth. I said those words without being able to stop them from pouring out.

"You seem real sure that Asher knows what's best." There was a sourness in his tone and I didn't blame him for it. Everything was still raw and new between us.

"I was just thinking is all. Not my business. I'm sorry. I don't know what your bills are or how much the farm makes for you all. You do. It's not my business."

He was quiet for a moment and I wondered if I'd said the wrong thing yet again. This was going to be difficult for a while. Maybe forever. Could I do this? Was this even fair to Steel?

He admitted, "I don't know what the farm brings in," and he didn't seem proud of that fact either.

"Oh," was all I said.

We rode in silence to the only seafood place in town. I fidgeted my hands and kept my gaze out the window like I'd never been here before. Part of me hoped to see Bray out there somewhere on the street. To assure me it hadn't been him in the truck. I really wanted to know that it wasn't. Then suddenly Steel said, "Asher does. And Bray. They help Momma with the finances. Asher did it until he left. Momma does most of it now, but Asher was so good at math she had him start helping when he turned seventeen. When he left for college, she let Bray step in. Someone had to step in. Bray was the best choice."

He didn't have to admit this to me. This was another thing about Steel to love and respect. He was honest, didn't lie to make himself look better, but even that couldn't change my heart. I wished it could. Even when my heart should've lied, it didn't.

"They're older," I replied simply to comfort him.

He nodded. "Yeah, but I care more about the place. Making it a real working farm. Turning more than just enough to pay the bills. I want to see it thrive. Give Momma some extra to put back into it. You know what I mean?"

I tilted my chin, but didn't say any more. Instead, my eyes suddenly found Asher. Like they always seemed to do. He was walking out of the hardware store with Hannah Watson stepping beside him. She was talking and smiling brightly, her face turning to gesture as they strolled, while Asher listened and took it all in. The small lift at the corners of his lips meant Hannah was making him truly smile, and Asher was liking whatever she was saying. Until this moment, I'd always liked Hannah. She was beautiful, smart and nice. But now I hoped she tripped over her pretty blue sandals and fell flat on her face. Or for a truck to hit her in the street. What was happening to me?

"Asher moved on that fast enough. The boss's daughter is already hanging on his arm. Not sure Denver was expecting that."

Why did Asher need another job anyway? That was silly. I suddenly agreed with Steel. There was no point in him working elsewhere with so much to do on their oen farm. Especially if it meant he was going to be around Hannah all the time. Wasn't she supposed to be off at school? Why was she traipsing the streets with Asher? Drooling and looking all pretty?

"I thought she went up north to college somewhere," I said

a little too loudly, trying to then soften my voice at the end, but you could still hear it sounded all wrong.

"She did. Guess she's home for the summer."

A summer romance.

My stomach turned sour.

I wasn't going to be able to eat anything now. Not a single bite.

Why did I have to see this? I wanted to see Bray, not Asher.

"Ready for lunch?" Steel asked as he parked the truck.

"Yeah," I replied with even less enthusiasm than before, unsure I'd be able to swallow even one fried shrimp after the scene I'd just witnessed in the street.

I watched as Asher walked out to his truck and Hannah climbed on the passenger side. They had ridden here together. They were headed somewhere together. Asher was supposed to be working. Why wasn't he working instead of gallivanting all over town with Hannah? My stomach clinched, jealousy dulling everything around me, even the air now smelling different to me. The sun looked less bright, the sky less blue, and my heart kept fracturing more and more. I didn't know that it could break any more. But it seemed it could.

chapter
SEVENTEEN

Asher Sutton

I HAD NO idea why I was at Jack's with Amber Fort. But after the day I had with Hannah flirting incessantly with me and my trying to make sure she understood we were just going to be friends, I needed a drink. A big one. Hannah wasn't taking the hint, though. When I walked into Jack's, Amber had been here all tanned up from working at the salon with her tits and legs on display and I figured I needed a distraction. Amber knew the score. She wasn't in it for the romance or promises of a forever. We'd messed around once in high school. She knew the drill.

Amber sat down on my lap as soon as I took a seat on the closest bar stool. "My day just got a helluva lot better," she drawled, leaning in to shove her cleavage in my face. I wished that I could say the same.

"Heard you were driving around with sweet Hannah Watson," she continued. This town had little to do but talk about people. I figured they'd have me and Hannah engaged by next week at this rate. Another reason to let Amber sit on my lap. Maybe enough people would see it and I'd just get labeled a manwhore instead.

"I'm working for Denver," I told her as if she didn't know this already.

She wrapped an arm over my shoulders and leaned in closer. "I heard that, but I also know you like your girls sweet. I figure it's about time you tried some naughty." I assumed she saw herself as the naughty in that sentence.

Vince Wallace and Todd Hyatt walked in and headed for a pool table. "Asher! Heard you were in town," Vince called out while walking over to me. I'd played football with both of them. Wasn't sure what either of then were doing now, though.

"Yeah, I'm home for a bit," I told him.

"I see you got some good hometown entertainment," he said grinning at Amber who just giggled.

I wasn't sure how to respond to that.

"Ash, man, saw you play this year on TV. It was fucking crazy to see. Kept telling the boys I used to play on the same field as you," Todd said as he took a beer from Jack's nephew Roy who was working the bar today.

That seemed to excite Amber because she managed to wrap herself tighter against me. I knew I could have just taken what she was offering all too happily. But I also knew I'd feel guilty later. Not sure why. Dixie was my brother's girlfriend. I'd been with other women since her. Something about being home and seeing her again made it all different.

"You're living the dream. Living the dream," Todd said with a wistfulness in his tone. He was my age, but he'd gotten married the week after high school graduation and his twin boys had been born the next month. That is all I knew about Todd.

"Good to have you home," Vince told me, then the two of them moved to the pool table.

Amber's thigh moved down between mine until she was pressing and rubbing it against my dick. "Want to go somewhere so I can kiss on that?" she offered.

Before I had to make a decision, the door opened again and Bray walked in. He became my excuse for telling her no. "Tap," was all that Bray said to Roy before walking to stand beside us and looking at me.

"You the only one here?"

"Yeah. The others are . . . out," I told him, not sure exactly where they all were.

"What up, Amber?" Bray asked, winking at Amber who squirmed in my lap some more. I was walking out of here if she started mentioning a threesome. I'd had enough women in the past who'd asked for one with one of my brothers and that shit was not happening. Ever.

"Trying to get this one to take me out to his truck," she said, pressing her body against mine some more.

"Good luck," he replied. He knew me too damn well. "You up for a game," Bray asked me.

"Yeah." I needed to do something other than let Amber rub all over me. The fact that my dick was hard didn't mean I wanted her. It meant it was being rubbed on and it was what a dick did. I patted her leg. "Let me up, babe." As soon as I said the words, her eyes lit up. Damn. I hadn't meant it as a term of endearment.

Suddenly, her lips were on mine and I decided to just go for it. To try and see if I wanted more. But I knew immediately that this wasn't something I could fake. Her body felt good, she had a great one, but this would only end up being one more pointless fuck.

Taking her by the waist, I moved her gently off me and stood up. It was then that my eyes locked with Dixie's. Her skin was pale and the raw pain in her eyes shook me to my core. I didn't want to hurt her. I never wanted to see her look at me like that again. I'd seen that look too many times in the past.

I forced my legs to move away from Amber before she did any more groping. "Rack 'em," I said to Bray, tearing my gaze off Dixie.

"She ain't worth it," Bray said under his breath.

"Yeah, she is," I replied. She was worth so much more than Bray would ever understand. He didn't love anyone like that. I doubted he ever would.

"Amber's hot," he said as if I needed that pointed out to me. I glanced back at Amber, wondering if I could go there. Lose myself in her, even if only for one night.

"I know. I'm trying to focus on that," I told him.

My head was so fucking messed up with Dixie being there, I had missed my other brothers walking into the bar. "I got the winner," Steel said all happy like he owned the damn world. He did. He had *my* world. He had my Dixie.

"So you'll be playing Bray. Nobody can beat his ass," Brent said with an amused smirk directed my way. He was right. Bray was the undefeated champion among us.

Although, at the moment, Bray looked wound up tight. He had that crazy look in his eyes he would get whenever his temper was about to flare up. Bray'd had anger issues since he was a little boy. He'd lose his shit in an instant and calming him down had never been easy. Dad had been good at it. But once Dad was gone, we never really knew how to do it. The older he got, the less it happened. But when it did, it was dangerous for everyone involved.

Momma said he needed to see a psychiatrist. Regularly. Bray said he had no use for a shrink. We all agreed he was wrong. He needed help controlling himself. I wasn't sure what the fuck had just set him off, but it was clearly boiling under the surface. He then turned to a blonde I knew he dated in high school and started flirting. She didn't know to stay away from that dangerous gleam in his eyes. He was going to use her as a distraction. But from what?

I turned to look at Brent to see if he noticed it, too, but he was leaving with Scarlet. As much as I didn't want to look at Steel, I did. I needed backup and soon. But Steel wasn't looking at Bray, either. He was smiling back at Dixie. *Shit.*

"Brent leaving?" Steel asked, then looked at me.

"Looks like it," I replied, giving him a pointed look, then shooting my eyes toward Bray to get his attention.

Steel frowned like he wasn't sure what I was trying to say. *Were they all blind?*

Bray slammed his stick down then and turned to stalk out of the bar. That caught Steel's attention and he was right behind me as I hurried for the door. Hell was about to break loose and I was afraid I had just figured out why. *Fuck.*

chapter
EIGHTEEN

Dixie Monroe

STEEL CURSED UNDER his breath and hurried after Asher. Both of them were now following Bray who had seemed angry. I must had missed something. I wasn't exactly sure what that was since all my focus had been on Asher. I was watching him to see if he looked at Amber anymore. It was ridiculous of me, but I had needed reassurance he wasn't really interested in her.

I followed behind Steel who seemed to have forgotten about me. Not that it mattered. Something else was obviously wrong. I wish Scarlet had stayed. Brent had been so determined to leave with her.

I had barely made it to the steps when Bray's voice rang through the parking lot, "Don't, Scar."

I squinted in the dark to see Scarlet pressed up against Brent's truck and Brent and her were obviously doing stuff. But the raw pain in Bray's voice stopped me in my tracks. Caused me to stop breathing. Because in that moment, I *knew*. I knew what I had feared was true after all. Had Steel and Asher known? They'd ran out of there like they did? Surely they weren't okay with this? Not when Asher was so determined that he couldn't be with me because of his brother.

"Come here, baby," Bray said. His tone was gentle yet demanding. My stomach turned. Oh, god. This was bad.

I stepped closer just as Scarlet looked up at Brent and said, "I'm sorry." Then she left his arms and rushed into the arms of his twin brother.

Asher moved then. Fast. "What the fuck," he roared. His voice was loud and full of fury. I'd never heard him so angry.

"Please tell me you're shitting me," Steel said moving to stand beside Asher. Like they were a united front, ready to take on Bray.

"Oh, shit, what have you done?" Dallas was here now, too. He was coming up from behind me. His boots hitting the gravel as he moved to stand with the others.

I'd feared this. Deep down, I think I knew it all along. Scarlet loved Bray. But I'd not wanted to believe she would do this to Brent.

"She's mine," Bray said, turning to look back at the brothers behind him, then back to his twin.

"What have you done?" Brent sounded like he'd been ripped in half. I knew how that felt. My heart broke for him.

"She's been mine. I wouldn't admit it and you kept pushing to get her to go out with you, so she did. I should have said something then. I didn't. I fucked up. But she's mine. She's been mine all along."

How could she do this? I understood loving one Sutton and being with another, but I'd never do this. Or was what I was doing even worse? Was this what it would feel like for Steel if I kept this up, knowing he'd never have my heart?

"Dixie, you need to take Scarlet," Asher's voice was loud and cold. His gaze locked on Bray. Daring him to say anything. He moved toward Bray. "Let her go with Dixie. We got shit to clear up," Asher wasn't asking. His voice was tight and hard.

"Scarlet," I said taking a step forward. I would do whatever they needed me to. I agreed with Asher. They all needed to deal with this on their own and Scarlet needed to leave. Her being there just made it all worse.

"Don't touch her," Bray growled as my hand touched her arm. In that moment, my heart skipped a beat from the sheer terror I felt. The look in Bray's eyes was that of a demon. Evil. Cruel. Nothing like his usual self at all.

Scarlet was startled by his words, too, and I jumped. Moved away fast. Something was wrong with him.

Dallas was there suddenly, pulling Scarlet back, just as Asher's fist slammed into Bray's face. Scarlet screamed. I screamed. I heard other screams.

"Don't ever fucking talk to her like that again," Asher's threat was full of his own anger. This was the first time I'd seen him like this, too. His fist landed again on Bray's face.

Scarlet was trying to break free from Dallas. She was screaming, "Stop! Please stop!" She was begging Asher to stop.

He was going to kill Bray. Or it looked that way, at least. Bray couldn't seem to get his head clear enough after each hit to do anything. None of the others were stopping Asher. He'd regret this. I knew him too well. If he truly hurt Bray, he'd never forgive himself. Dallas was so busy holding Scarlet, so I was able to go to Asher. I grabbed his arm before he swung again.

"Asher, don't," I said hoping he could hear me over Scarlet's screaming. He did. He stilled. Bray began wiping the blood running from his nose.

"Back up, Dixie," Asher said, not looking at me. His glare remained fixed on Bray.

Bray moved then. But not toward Asher. He moved toward Scarlet. "Let. Her. Go."

Dallas shook his head. "Seriously, Bray, you got some shit to work out. She needs to leave with Dixie."

Asher finally looked at me. "Step away from this. If you're hurt, I'll end up killing him." He wasn't exaggerating. That wasn't a threat. He was serious. I moved back then. I wasn't sure how I felt about that. Knowing he'd physically hurt his brother over me.

"You need to leave with Dixie. And Dallas needs to take you both home," Asher told Scarlet. I looked at her pleadingly. She needed to listen to him. This was only getting worse with her being there.

"Okay," Scarlet agreed, "but don't hurt him again. I did this. It was all me. I played games and caused this. I just wanted him . . ." She didn't finish. She'd said enough right there. Enough to cause damage. Was this what Asher didn't want to happen between him and Steel?

Asher swore again and shook his head, then pointed to Dallas's truck. "Take 'em home. Then you need to come back."

Dallas nodded. No one was arguing with Asher. "Let's go," he said to both of us and I walked over to stand beside Scarlet. Dallas let her go and put a hand on both our shoulders. "My truck," he said in a low voice.

Scarlet looked at me then. She was scared and she was sorry. I could read the regret in her eyes. But she also was worried about me. Because of Asher's actions. He hadn't hit Bray over Scarlet. He'd hit him because of how he spoke to me. But what did I do with that? I couldn't hope. After tonight, after this, he'd never do the same to his brother. But then, I wouldn't either. I'd end things before that ever happened. It was what Scarlet should have done in the first place. I turned back to see all of them squared off, bodies tense, and blue lights coming down the road. The cops had been called. Wouldn't be the first time the Sutton boys were greeted by the police. It was a good thing. Otherwise none of them might survive the night.

chapter
NINETEEN

Bray Sutton

BRENT'S TRUCK WAS parked out by the barn when I finally came home. So was Asher's and Steele's. Only the old rusted farm truck was missing. I headed for the barn, not sure what I was about to face. There was a good chance they would all take turns beating the shit out of me.

When Brent would be ready to listen, I would find a way to explain it to him. But if he needed to hit me until his hand was bruised, I'd let him. I owed him that much. I handled this wrong. I wouldn't apologize for needing Scarlet. That was something I wasn't going to do. Because I needed her. I hadn't been sure that I could ever feel any real emotion until Scarlet managed to get under my skin and wedge herself firmly in my heart. It was like I had walked through life without understanding passion, jealousy or even love . . . before her. I'd only known anger. It was a numbness I never wanted to live with again.

Scarlet changed all that for me. Maybe I was obsessed. Fuck, maybe I needed a new medication. But I needed to touch Scarlet and feel her to experience real pleasure. She gave me something I didn't know existed and now I wasn't willing to let that go. Not even for my brother.

I opened the barn door and Asher turned to look at me. He was the only one in there. And he was going to hand my ass to me now that I was home. I was prepared for that. As long as I had Scarlet. As long as she was mine, I would happily take whatever they wanted to give me.

"He's out helping Steel," Asher informed me.

I nodded. I wasn't sure what he thought I should do. Go find him? He'd be back soon enough. I turned to walk back out of the barn. I needed a shower. Sleeping outside in the back of my truck all night hadn't left me smelling good. I could still smell Scarlet and sex on my hands, too. I didn't want to wash her off, but I also knew the sex smell would have told my brothers more than any of them needed or wanted to know.

"She came by to see him," Asher said just before I walked out the door.

I froze. I didn't want Scarlet coming to see Brent or anyone else for that matter. I had unleashed some kind of fucking monster last night when I'd allowed myself to lay claim to her. My hands clenched tightly into fists at my side at the thought of her apologizing to Brent.

"When," I bit out through my teeth.

"About three hours ago," Asher replied.

I took a deep breath through my nose and tried like hell to calm the fuck down. "What did she say?"

"She said she'd been selfish and she was sorry," Asher informed me.

My heart slammed against my chest and I grabbed the door-frame to keep from putting my fist through a wall. "Did he touch her?" If he had, I wouldn't be able to control myself.

"No. She didn't get within ten feet of him when she spoke to him," he said slowly. "Bray, what the hell is wrong with you? You're acting like someone fucked your girlfriend. Not the other way around."

I ripped off the door facing and tossed it aside, before glaring back at Asher. "She's mine."

Asher raised his eyebrows. "She was Brent's. You didn't respect that."

"*No*," I roared, taking a step toward him. "She was *always* mine."

Asher studied me, but he didn't move. He didn't even flinch. "What's happened to you?"

How would I explain to him, to any of them, how Scarlet made me feel? What she gave me. I felt my body begin to shake.

"You okay . . . what's wrong? Look at me, Bray," the concern in Asher's voice snapped me out of the panic that was starting to squeeze my lungs. I had to find Scarlet. I needed her to touch me. To ease this.

"I gotta go," I said before turning and stalking back to my truck. Getting to Scarlet was all what I needed first. Everything else could wait. She'd been here and she'd talked to Brent. I had to know what he said to her. I needed her to tell me it was still me she wanted.

The slamming of a car door caught my attention and I turned to see Dixie standing beside her car with tears streaming down her face.

"What's wrong?" Asher called out as he walked past me hell bent on getting to Dixie.

"Careful, bro. She belongs to Steel," I said causing him to stop and swing a warning glare toward me.

Didn't feel so good when someone told you your woman was someone else's, did it? Maybe he'd remember that next time.

"She's gone," Dixie said looking at me instead of Asher.

My lungs ceased up and my pulse sped up. The world around me faded away. "No," was all I could get out.

Dixie looked at Asher and covered her mouth on a sob. "She left me a note. She said she wasn't her mother. She had to fix what she'd done."

No. No. *No.*

Scarlet was not gone. She didn't leave me. She knew she couldn't leave me. I made it very clear to her last night.

"*No!*" My voice didn't even sound like mine. I was moving toward Dixie now. I had to stop her from saying any more lies.

Asher was in my face and he shoved me back until I stumbled. "Get a hold of yourself. Jesus! You've lost your mind. What is fucking wrong with you?"

"*No!*" I yelled at the top of my lungs again, letting all the fear and panic that was trying to take hold of me grip me even tighter.

"Oh, fuck," Asher's voice was out there somewhere. I heard it but I couldn't focus on what he was saying.

"Go find Steel."

"It's his meds. Shit, I should have realized this sooner."

"What meds?"

"They aren't working."

"Asher, what meds?"

Their voices faded out completely until it was all black. And I roared with the pain taking over my chest. She'd left me. I was hollow again.

chapter
TWENTY

Asher Sutton

WHEN BRAY REFUSED to go to counseling over his temper issues, the doctor prescribed an antidepressant he said helped with anger management. It had. A lot. It kept Bray calm. For the past five years, he rarely ever lost his temper. He was laid back and a smartass. I should have noticed he'd been different since I got home. There was no telling how long he'd been off them. He'd covered it up well. Until two nights ago.

Scarlet's leaving was for the best. I knew Dixie was going to miss her and I hated that for her, but my brothers needed time. If I had to drag Bray to a counselor and sit there with him twice a week, I was prepared to do it. There was something deep inside him none of us knew how to help him overcome. Something that haunted him. Controlled him. He needed help. More than a damn pill could do.

We'd kept his issue and the fact he needed medication for it from the others. Only I knew. Momma had asked me to talk him into taking it in the beginning. She couldn't get him to do it. I'd somehow managed to convince him he needed them. But with me gone, he'd decided to go off them. I knew that after this, I wasn't going to be able to return to Florida. I'd go back for a small break, but I was needed here. Momma would tell me I wasn't, that I should go live my life, but I knew better. The boys needed me. Momma needed me. I shouldn't have left to begin with.

"Asher, I need you to deliver a load to Luke Monroe, if you will." Denver called out from the back door of Watson's Feed and Seed. I was unloading a truck and restocking. The sun was hot as hell and normally I liked doing deliveries. But not this time. Not to Luke Monroe's. Not today. Not after the other night. Avoiding Dixie was the only way I managed to stay sane. In the last forty-eight hours, I had to deal with her more than I could bare because it made me miss her even more. Our bond was still there. Even when hell was breaking loose, it was there. However, telling my boss I wasn't going to do my job because of a girl wasn't exactly an option. I swore under my breath and called back, "Okay, what's he need?"

"Hannah is bringing you the list. She's the one who took the order."

And this just kept getting better and better. Hannah liked having an excuse to come out here and see me. If she didn't have an order for me, she brought me a drink. It was nice of her to do that, but I knew by the way she was smiling and giggling that it wasn't because she thought I was thirsty. Hannah wanted us to become more. She wasn't hard on the eyes and unlike some of the other girls in town, she was also intelligent and ambitious. I'd heard all about her plans after college. Hannah was organized, even more so than me, she liked current events, and chatted on a lot about politics. I listened, but didn't say much. She had a nice voice, and if only briefly, she'd distracted me from my thoughts of Dixie. But it was short-lived.

I wiped my forehead with the towel I kept tucked in my pocket. When sweat got into my eyes, with dirt mixed in, it burned like a motherfucker. Before I could prepare myself for going to Luke's, Hannah came strutting to the back. Her navy shorts were showing every inch of her legs. One centimeter shorter and her rounded ass cheeks would peep out for all to see. The pale yellow tank top she was wearing was the only thing covering her tits. No bra. I wondered why Denver let her dress that way. Display herself like that.

"Need help loading this stuff," she asked as she all but bounced walking toward me, grinning and selling it.

"Thanks, but I got it," I replied.

She always smiled, perennially happy about life, which I envied and often wondered what that felt like. But she wasn't dressed for manual labor. She never was, yet she always offered to help me.

"I can ride with you," she said, as if she was being helpful.

Taking Hannah with me would keep me from being alone while going to Dixie's for the first time since this all happened. But I had demons to face and needed the quiet of my truck to prepare myself mentally. Dixie was very likely going to marry Steel. I had to accept that. Move on, though I wasn't sure yet how I was going to do that. Although Bray's reaction wasn't healthy or normal, I understood his desperation. I felt the same way. I just reacted differently.

"I'm sure you're needed at the front desk. I got this. But thanks," I told her as gently as I could. She moved closer and closer every time she rode with me. I was concerned Hannah would be plastering herself up against me soon. Again, she was easy on the eyes and it wasn't hard having her pressed against my body that way. I just wasn't ready. As much as I wished I was, I wasn't, but she kept trying anyway. I respected her enough not to use her. I didn't think she saw it that way. That's what worried me most.

"I'd rather be with you," she replied, her voice dropping into a husky tone that was intended to be sexy. She wasn't trying to be subtle at all as she rubbed her chest against my left arm.

I stepped back and reached for a bag of feed. I wasn't even sure what kind I was holding. "Uh, Hannah, I'm flattered. But we both work for your dad and I don't think that, uh, well . . ." I really sucked at this "I think this is a bad idea."

She pouted. Looked damn good pouting, too. But not good enough to make me forget where I'd be going with her.

"I just knew going to the Monroe's might be tough on you. I wanted to be there for support, if you needed any . . . support. I can think of a few ways I could help ease any ache . . . or suffering that going there might cause you."

Her eyes went to my cock as she spoke. I'd be lying if I said I didn't consider it. I was a man, but I didn't hesitate when I said, "Thanks Hannah, but it's best if we keep this a friend thing if that's okay with you?"

She sighed and dropped the seductive gaze she'd been giving me. She looked more like old Hannah now. Sweet, kind Hannah, but in fewer clothes than she'd been wearing that very first day when I started working there. Her clothing had gotten skimpier and skimpier by the day, and by the end of next week, if she continued at her current pace, Hannah would be coming to work naked. Maybe her daddy would notice then.

"You're always going to love Dixie Monroe, aren't you, Asher Sutton?" She wasn't talking in her sultry voice anymore. She was back to being herself. I thought about denying it, but I knew Hannah wouldn't tell anyone, no matter my response. It would stay between us and I needed to say it, admit it to someone. Anyone.

"Yeah, I will, but I let her go, and she moved on."

She frowned. "Why did you break up with her? That's a

mystery no one has ever understood."

"It's complicated." I wasn't telling anyone that. Not Hannah. Not a fucking soul.

She nodded as if she understood, when I knew she didn't, couldn't and wouldn't. "Okay, Asher, I get it. But when you're tired of seeing her with your brother and you're ready to move on to something else, don't forget me. I can wait."

"If that day ever comes, you'll be first I call."

That brought a smile to her face. I liked seeing her smile. I didn't want to think I'd been the one to take her ever-present smile away. "I could still go with you for moral support. As a fellow employee."

I considered it. Having Hannah with me would've made it less awkward, but then again, it could've made things even more awkward, too. I shook my head. "Not this time. This is something I need to get over and deal with . . . but thank you for asking, Hannah."

She shrugged her shoulders. "Okay, good luck, then."

"Thanks." Best thing I could have hoped for was for Dixie not to be home. Then I could unload, talk to Luke about work, and leave as quickly as possible.

Loading the truck didn't take me long. I was on the road and headed to the Monroe's in about twenty minutes. Had Hannah been sitting in the seat beside me, I might have felt a false sense of security. But that was all it would've been. No matter who was there, I had to face them eventually, see this through. And if Dixie was there, then I'd have to talk to her. Talk to her like my brother's girlfriend. Accept what I said and what had to be, knowing she loved me, too. That was the hardest part. Knowing that my heart wasn't the only one I broke. If there had been a way to save Steel in all this, I would've done it, but I didn't see any other way to escape the truth.

Pulling the truck onto the dirt road that ran beside Luke's big barn, I saw only his truck sitting there. Relieved by that, I parked and jumped down. I planned on making some small talk, unload the truck, and be gone in no time at all.

"I can help you unload that, Asher." Dixie's sweet, southern drawl stopped me in my tracks. I froze like a blizzard had hit me.

Motherfucking shit.

chapter
TWENTY-ONE

Dixie Monroe

I'D HEARD DADDY on the phone placing his order from Watson's Feed and Seed. He didn't know that Asher was likely to be delivering the order for them. I did. I knew it would be him. When Momma said that she had lunch ready, I told him to go on and eat with her, that I'd go out to the barn in case the delivery came. Oddly enough, he seemed fine with that. I expected it to be harder. He trusted me, but he was fatherly suspicious, as all good fathers were.

Asher's back was still to me. He hadn't turned around. He'd been expecting my dad and was obviously surprised when I was the one waiting there. I was relieved Hannah Watson didn't climb from the truck. I wasn't sure what my plan would have been if she'd been there with him. I was only focused on Asher, on speaking to him alone, even though I knew this was wrong. Even if he'd said it was over between us, I wanted to hear his voice again. See if it was truly over between us.

"Dad's eating lunch," I said, hoping he'd look at me.

His shoulders sagged and I felt somewhat guilty. The last two days had been hard on him. Having Scarlet rip Bray and Brent apart had been tough on all of them. He slowly turned to face me, "I'm having a hard time believing your daddy left you out here to take this delivery from me."

Nonchalantly, I lifted my left shoulder. "He might not have known you worked for Denver."

Asher shook his head and turned his gaze to the house. "Best I unload this and be on my way."

He didn't want to look at me. I knew that. Hated it even more. Did he sense desperation in my voice? Did he think that after the other night I expected more? That his showing how he felt for me by beating Bray's face in would confuse me. Well, it did. But it also showed me that Asher was never going to hurt Steel. I had other plans. Another idea.

"We were friends once," I said, knowing we could never actually be friends. That was no longer possible.

"No, Dix, we weren't. I always wanted you. Never thought of you as a friend."

I wanted to smile at that. It was something. But I didn't smile. I didn't let him see how much I liked hearing it because he'd just unload and run. I had to maintain some sort of wall, a barrier between us to keep him here, talking to me.

"I saw you with Hannah. Y'all dating?" I wasn't sure what had gotten into me today, but I couldn't shut up, had to say everything I was thinking. Jealousy was killing me.

"You also saw me with Amber. You're not asking about her."

"I know you'd never really feel anything for Amber. Hannah is different. You could love her."

"I work with her. She's a friend."

They worked together. She saw him every day. Eventually that could lead to more. "She's really pretty," I replied. The words just kept spewing from my mouth.

"Yeah, she is," he said.

Having him agree with me on that didn't feel good at all. I continued with the stupid questions, "She likes you?" It sounded like a question but I meant it as a statement.

He shrugged. "Not important, is it, Dix? Why are you doing this?"

Everything about him was important to me. Vital, even. The fact that my heart ached for him every day and I felt empty and hollow inside mattered because this was what my life had become. I replied before I could stop myself, "Because, Asher . . . I love you."

He closed his eyes tightly, his hands fisting at his sides. "Dixie, for the love of God, please stop. I can't do this with you. I can't listen to this or do anything about it. If I could, don't you get that I would?"

The pain etched on his face, in his eyes, told me he was hurting too. And I was only making it worse. "I can't stay with Steel. It's not right. It feels . . . wrong to pretend. I keep pretending to love him when I'm in love with someone else. Always have been."

Asher sighed, his breaths heavy now. He was searching for a response. "Even if you don't stay with Steel, Dixie, I just can't. He's my brother. You saw what happened with Bray and Brent."

I knew this already. But something inside me had to try one more time. It was wrong and cruel of me, but I had to try. I knew our situation was different. Bray and Scarlet had played with Brent's emotions by using him to make the other jealous. I'd never done that to Steel. I never would. I was only guilty of loving Asher too much. But my heart knew what it wanted. Did that make me a bad person? I couldn't find it in myself to care. My heart refused to let him go.

"I can help unload," I said again. There was nothing else to say. I'd help him. Endure the pain of having him near and not be his, but he would be close. That would be enough.

"Why don't you go and let your dad know I'm here? I'll unload and then be on my way." He said all that without once looking in my direction. The summer sun made his hair appear lighter than it was, highlighting its thick strands. His skin was tanned and I knew from summers past it would only get darker with time. The broad shoulders that made the taught fabric of his shirt cling to his skin had once been mine, to grip, hold onto, but now they weren't mine to touch anymore. Nothing about Asher Sutton belonged to me anymore. All I had left were my memories. Every look, every touch, every kiss, everything he ever said to me. You could have put me in a box, thrown away the key, fed me enough just to keep me alive, and even after years had passed, I would have recognized his voice anywhere.

"Okay," I replied and I did what I had to do at that moment. I walked away from the boy I'd loved and the man I couldn't forget.

Part of me hoped he'd stop me, call out to me asking me to turn around. But I knew better. Where I was weak and selfish, Asher was strong and selfless, keeping his word regardless of how he felt. He'd put his brother first, before anything else he wanted. I couldn't hate him for that. He was being the good guy. And I was behaving like the villain.

Climbing the few short steps on my porch, I inhaled deeply, staring bravely at the large wooden door closed in front of me. I had to go inside and act like my heart wasn't breaking into pieces. Let my dad know the delivery had come, then make some excuse to skip lunch, and head straight to my bedroom to hide.

Once upon a time, Asher had kissed me on these steps. Countless nights I'd sat here and waited for him to come. On even more lonely nights, I'd watched for his truck to pass, wondering why he didn't want me anymore and what I had done to lose him.

This porch, these steps held more memories than I could

count. I walked to the door, and put a brave smile on my face, one I didn't feel and hadn't truly felt in a very long time. I knew my parents would be in the kitchen. I could have called out, masked the pain in my voice, and just kept walking to my room. But I had to face my fears.

"Delivery came. It's all good." I hoped there would be no questions.

"Did it get unloaded?" Dad asked.

"Yes, sir."

"Good. Thank you."

"You're welcome," I replied, moving swiftly toward the stairs, almost escaping the next question.

"You coming to eat?" Momma asked. "It's on the table, dear."

I expected it. Knew it was coming. I replied, "Not hungry yet. Ate breakfast too late. I'm going to go read." Today was my day off from the hair and tanning salon where I worked. I was the receptionist and I washed all the towels, too. Being lazy around the house on my days off was more acceptable now since I started working five days a week. The salon was closed on Sundays so I didn't work then, spending those days reading as much as I could. I tried to keep to myself, though Steel took a lot of my free time. I knew I wouldn't have felt that way had I loved him truly.

Once I was safely inside my room, I sank down on the bed and fell backwards. Staring at the ceiling, I faced the reality of what I had to do. I had to break up with Steel. Not because it would change anything with Asher—because it wouldn't, it was set in stone—but because I just couldn't do this to Steel anymore. He was a good guy, a great guy, and he deserved a girl who would love him for the amazing man that he was. That wasn't me. It never would be. I'd already let this go too far.

I wasn't proud of myself or my actions. But that didn't mean I couldn't change them. Do the right thing and get strong enough to move on. Find a life outside of this town, one without a Sutton boy by my side. Asher was right about one thing. I wasn't meant for a Sutton boy.

chapter
TWENTY-TWO

Asher Sutton

"WHERE THE FUCK you been?" Dallas asked as I walked into the house. I knew by his language Momma wasn't inside, or he would've paid dearly for that.

"Work," I replied moving past him, heading to the fridge to get a glass of sweet tea and some food. I'd skipped my lunch break because Hannah had asked me to go with her. I lied and said I'd brought a sandwich, that I'd scarf it down and keep on working.

Grabbing some cold fried chicken, half an apple pie, cheddar cheese and the leftover biscuits, I set the banquet on the table and closed the door.

"You gonna share?" Dallas asked with a grin.

"No. Get your own."

"I would, but you just cleaned out the damn fridge."

I began slicing some cheese to go with my biscuits and took a tomato from the window seal. I knifed the stem head and cut it down the middle. After talking to Dixie, having had to say the things she needed to hear, I just wanted to be left alone. I wasn't in the mood for my little brother's smart mouth.

"Hey, slice me some tomato, too. Tomato, cheese and biscuits sound good. I'm starving," Steel said as the screen door slammed shut behind him. "Oh, hot damn! There's some chicken left, too."

"He's not sharing," Dallas chimed in before I could reply. "He's come in scowling and angry, determined to eat us out of house and home, which you can see is all on the table before you."

"Everything okay?" was Steel's immediate response. He was assuming this was about Bray, who was still locked in his room, heavily medicated. I sliced another tomato, put it on a plate, then turned to hand it to Steel.

"I'm fine. Just hungry. Didn't eat all day. Take a couple of biscuits if you want. But the chicken, that's all mine."

Steel took the plate of tomato from me and sat down at the table. His gaze remained stuck on me, studying me, weighing my mood by my movements. It was hard having any secrets with a house full of nosey ass brothers. I'd been gone so long I forgot what this was like. Having someone always there watching you. Paying attention to your every mood. At school, no one cared. I could close off and get drunk all alone. No one ever questioned it. Here, that was impossible.

Steel asked, "Why didn't you eat at work? Denver not give you a lunch break?"

"Yeah, he does, worked through it."

"Then that's your own fucking fault. Share the chicken," Dallas replied, leaning over the table to grab a drumstick. I clutched his wrist and glared at him.

"I'm not in the mood," I warned him. "Get your own goddamn food." As the last word fell from my mouth, the screen door opened again and Brent walked in. He had been working outside since early this morning, ignoring Bray locked away in his room and the fact Scarlet had left town.

"Jesus. Y'all fighting over food?"

I tried to act like everything was normal for him. Not treat him with kid gloves like everyone else was doing. He obviously didn't want to be treated that way. "No. This fucker won't leave my lunch alone."

"It's four thirty in the afternoon. That ain't lunch," was Brent's response.

"He didn't eat lunch. Now he's all pissy. Hoarding the food like a king." Dallas drawled and leaned back in his chair, smirking after saying it. "Just tell us why you didn't eat and I promise I'll leave you alone."

There had been times at college I missed this. My brothers, a full house, people who cared, but this wasn't one of those times. Right now, I was missing my privacy. Something this bunch knew nothing about. Currently, what I wanted was to be treated as a leper and avoided like the plague.

I put the chicken breast down with more force than necessary, looking up at three pairs of all too similar eyes, all directly focused on me. They were all waiting on my response. Nosey bastards. They had to know.

"Hannah. That's why I didn't eat. She won't leave me the hell alone. Now will you all let me fucking eat?" I was louder than necessary, but frustrated about being interrogated by them.

"So she held you down during your lunch break? Woman rode you? Wouldn't let you eat? If that's the case, I don't blame you for not eating. That's one hot piece of ass. Always thought she was a little uppity and superior, with her honor roll scholarship shit. But damn, those can be the wildest ones . . . did she happen to suck your dick?"

I stared at Dallas. When had my little brother turned into a complete dick?

"Don't think that's what happened," Steel said.

I shook my head. "No, it's not." I then took another bite of chicken.

"Okay, wait, you didn't bang Hannah?" Dallas asked.

My patience was running thin. I decided to eat in my room. Momma could bitch at me. I'd listen and apologize. That was better than this. Lifting my plate in one hand with my mason jar of tea firmly clasped in the other, I headed toward the stairs leading up to my room to escape my brothers' inquisition.

"You can't take food to your room." Dallas's tone was amused and playful.

"I don't give a fuck," I replied, slamming the door behind me, then locking it in place. They'd follow me, or at least Dallas would try just to see how far he could push me.

I heard his laughter and Steel saying something in a low, rumbling tone. I didn't try to listen. I sat down on the top step and finished my meal in silence. If I ate fast enough, I could get all evidence of it back to the kitchen before Momma returned. She was outside in the garden. Of course, that meant more taunting from Dallas. I'd rather just deal with Momma.

I replayed Dixie's voice in my mind again and again, her words to me, how happy I once made her. I hated hurting her, causing her any type of pain. I wished she'd understand that every time I pushed her back, every time I had to put her at a safe distance from me, my very being was being torn into shreds. This wasn't easy for me. From the moment I found those letters in that box, my life lost its meaning. I was drained of any joy and couldn't be filled again. The emptiness now seemed to be permanent.

The twisted guilt I'd lived with for the past three years was gone, but the ache of losing Dixie was still there. She wasn't the last girl I'd been with, but she'd been the only one that mattered. The only face I saw. No one made me feel complete like she had.

No one made me want to plan my forever, except her, only my Dixie. I thought that maybe with time there would be someone else to take her place, but all I realized in the end was that once you'd found perfection, everything else paled by comparison. A puzzle piece would forever be missing from your soul.

chapter
TWENTY-THREE

Dixie Monroe

WHILE STARING OUT the kitchen window, I poured myself a third cup of coffee. Sleep hadn't come last night. Not even a few seconds of it. My guilt kept me wide awake. I wasn't being fair to Steel. I'd known that before, but had let him convince me to stay with him because he honestly thought I could forget Asher one day. He thought we had a chance. I had to stop letting him think that. I cared about him, I wanted him to be loved the way he loved other people, completely, without hesitation. He was a good guy and should have it all. I was too fractured, too broken for him. Even though he refused to see it.

Telling him all this would not be easy. I knew that no matter how prepared I got, he was going to try and stop me. Convince me not to do this. I had to be strong or I'd continue hurting him forever. He'd hate me, all the Suttons would, especially now on the heels of what happened with Bray and Scarlet, but I couldn't just keep finding reasons to wait. I had to do this now. I had to end it so that he could move on.

Three long gulps and I finished the cup. I didn't even taste it. I'd drank it for the caffeine and the mental focus I needed for the task ahead. What I had to do wouldn't change anything with Asher. After yesterday, I knew that. He had decided that he could never be with me, and knowing he didn't love me the way I loved him would always sting deeply.

"You're up early. You don't have to be at work for another two hours," Mom said, yawning. She searched my face. It was six in the morning, and I'd been drinking coffee since five.

"I couldn't sleep," I replied, though I knew she knew that.

She came up behind me, wrapping her arms around my waist and resting her chin on my shoulder. "It isn't easy to do what's right. But you know that already."

Without me even telling her, she knew. Saw it all and read my heart. Tears stung my eyes because my mother expected me to do the right thing. To let Steel go, be truthful about it all, and she'd been waiting all along for me to do that.

"One day, there will be another man. Asher Sutton will become a memory. You won't ever forget him, but you will heal and move on. It's how the world works, honey. Though I know it's hard to see that now."

The idea of loving anyone else more than Asher seemed as heartbreaking as it was impossible to accept right now. "I don't know about that," I replied sullenly.

Again, Mom squeezed me tight. "You're young, life is rarely decided at eighteen years of age. We don't give our hearts away at fifteen, never to love again."

That was where she was wrong. I replied, "Thirteen. I gave it away at thirteen."

With a sigh, she kissed my temple, "Oh, Dixie, there's a big ol' world out there. One you've yet to explore. There's so many beautiful experiences that yet lie ahead of you. Trust me, sweetheart, if Asher Sutton was meant to be your only love, then it would've happened that way."

I closed my eyes. Fought back the tears. "I don't want to think it's over."

"The future is a funny thing. It may lead you around the world and bring you right back where you started."

I wiped away a single tear that had escaped. "Steel isn't going to be easy. He'll fight this. Try to stop me."

Mom ran her hand over my hair brushing it out of my face. "That's because you're beautiful and smart, loving and kind. No man will ever want to let that go, not without a fight."

Asher did. He let me go without a fight.

I didn't say the words aloud. Though they were there, always would be. It would be hard for me to truly trust enough to love again, the way I'd loved Asher. If that were even possible. If mom was right and someone else came along one day, would my heart be whole by then? I didn't think it could ever happen.

"Let me feed you before you go," she said, patting my arm and releasing her hold of me.

I couldn't eat. My stomach was in knots. "No, I'm not hungry. I have to do this now . . . before I back out. It has to be stopped."

"You've got to work all day. You need something in your stomach," she argued.

"I'll get something during my lunch break."

She didn't look convinced. "I'll bring you a late breakfast when I run to Harrods to get my vitamins."

Arguing with her was pointless. I nodded and considered another cup of coffee, but the queasiness in my stomach stopped me. I sat the cup down and gave Mom a hug. "Thanks. I love you," I said.

She rubbed my back, "I love you more. Never forget that."

I knew she was someone who would stay, make my dad happy, from the first time she said those words to me as a child. She made us a family again. She made us whole.

I grabbed my purse and headed for the door. "Here, at least take this protein bar," Mom said, following behind me and holding a peanut butter Cliff Bar in her hand.

I took it and thanked her, hoping to have an appetite later. She kissed my cheek one more time. I could see the love and worry for me on her face. The concern shining in her eyes.

When outside, I took a deep breath. This was going to be hard, but I could do it. Steel would be up and in the barn with his first cup of coffee by now. I wasn't sure when Asher went to work, though that might complicate things. But I knew he would avoid me at all costs, and today, I needed that.

The drive down to their house was short, but I used it to prepare myself for every argument Steel would throw my way. Hurting him was the last thing I wanted to do, but continuing to make Steel believe we had a chance was wrong and selfish of me. I didn't like being the villain, but I'd made my bed. Now I just needed to lie in it.

I parked at the barn. Didn't walk past their house. This was stressful enough without the other Sutton boys getting involved in our talk. I closed my door gently, in case anyone was still sleeping, the short distance from my car to the barn covered in a matter of seconds. It still felt like the longest walk of my life.

Steel was there like I knew he would be. He was good at what he did, dependable, hard-working, staying as long as it was needed, and often remaining after everyone else had left for the day. He deserved so much more than I was ever capable of giving him. I stepped inside and he turned immediately, the heavy barn door creaking with my entrance. The cup of coffee in his hand was a familiar sight. He was just as I had pictured him there—dressed

for hard work, knowing what he had to do, his hair roughed
slightly from sleep.

"Well, good morning," he said, with a slow lazy smile. He
wasn't fully awake yet. Not enough caffeine.

"Hey," I replied, hating every word before I even said them.

Straightaway, he sensed my mood. He was smart, observant
like that. I had to act fast, "Steel, let me talk first. Please? I want
to say my peace. I didn't come here to argue."

He thought about it. Wanted to say more. It was all there in
the way he was looking at me, but Steel remained silent because
I'd asked. Another reason to love him. Another reason to let him
go. I spoke again, "I can't continue doing this. It's unfair to you.
I'll love him until the day I die. I accept that. You're a wonderful
man. Someone who should have a girl on his arm who loves you
as deeply as you love her . . . but I'll never be that girl . . . I'm
damaged . . . I need you to understand that . . . Steel, you have
to let me go."

I'd planned on saying more, my ramblings making me lose my
train of thought and forget what I wanted to say. But I spoke the
truth. I said the facts, and now I had to give Steel time to respond.
His eyes held the disappointment and hurt I knew would come
from this. I expected that, but seeing it was difficult to witness.
Knowing he was happy when I first walked in, and that only I was
responsible for taking that away from him.

He sat his cup down on a shelf. Made a study of the ground
at his feet. I waited some more, wondering what he was thinking.
Would he fight this? Should I have said more? I kept questioning
everything I had said, thinking I could have said it better.

He suddenly replied, "That's it, then. I tried. I gave it my
best, but never got the same from you. Knew that. Forgave you
for it time and time again. But I held out hope that things would
change. If I was there for you, loved you hard enough, became

what you needed . . . that it would be enough. That I would be enough. But you're spoiled, want what you can't have. What I offered would have never been good enough . . . and that makes you not good enough for me. I want more, I want a woman who knows her own mind, can find her own damn happiness without a man's help . . . and that will never be you. So go on, Dixie, leave and don't come back. You want Asher, but he will never want you in return. He's moved on with his life. Now go waste the rest of yours on a pointless, empty dream."

Although I saw Steel Sutton standing before me and heard the words coming from his mouth, I was having a hard time believing he was saying such cruel, hurtful things to me, no matter how much I deserved them.

"Don't stand there and look all hurt and offended. What did you expect from me? Tears? Hell no, Dixie! I'm done trying to make you love me. If this is what you want, then that's what you can have. I just ask one final thing of you. Leave the diamond ring I gave you. It was meant for a woman who is worth it and deserves to wear it. That isn't you."

I had the ring in my pocket. That was what I'd planned to do, anyway. But I didn't imagine it happening this way. I pulled it out just as Steel took a step toward me and extended his hand between us, his palm up and his fingers twitching with impatience. The glare in his eyes was so foreign to me. The Steel I knew was gone and a cruel, heartless man had taken his place. And that man was reaching for his ring. I placed it in his hand, his fingers closing on it quickly as if I would take it back and run. He then said, "You can go now."

Thosee four words were filled with so much hate and disdain, that my legs almost gave out on me. I stumbled, but forced myself to draw strength from within, turning away, and sprinting from the barn and the monsters I had created.

chapter
TWENTY-FOUR

Asher Sutton

JOE GREEN MADE wooden lawn furniture. It was a popular item in Malroy and the only place you could buy it was Denver's. Today, I'd been going back and forth to Joe's to get the chairs, tables, and front porch swings that he'd made for the summer season. Hannah waited on me out front to deliver every load. She was showing me where to display them. That was her job, other than answering the phone and working the entrance of the business. She handled the design of the store, the placement of the items they sold, and stuff like that.

I was on my last load when Dallas's truck pulled in. Hannah noticed him first. She was moving a table around, to put a pot with some fancy ass flowers inside it, hoping to draw customers' attention. Dallas wouldn't be coming to see me unless there was a problem. He'd have me bring something home if we needed it at the house. No reason to come pick it up. I wiped the sweat from my forehead with my towel, tucking it back in my pocket, and hopping down from the bed of the truck just as he was headed my way.

"That your youngest brother?" Hannah asked, squinting against the sun.

I replied, "Yeah, give me a minute," walking toward him. My first thoughts, of course, went to Momma. I was the worrier in the bunch.

"Take your time," Hannah called after me, though I was too focused on Dallas to even care. The frown on his face meant this was about an annoyance rather than a problem. It couldn't be Momma. I sighed with relief. "You seen Steel?" he asked.

"No, why, should I?"

Dallas shook his head and said, "Naw, just thought maybe he'd come looking for you. He's been gone since Dixie came by this morning. She drove off and he left shortly after, slamming his door, then spinning his wheels so hard, gravel went flying all over the place. I was headed out to hit the bag some before work when I saw it all. Momma said to give him some time, then go looking for him. I figure he's a big boy and can handle his shit, but fuck if I'm gonna tell Momma that. A world of hurt would rain down on me."

I knew this was coming after Dixie had talked to me yesterday. She did the right thing and I was glad, though I knew Steel was crushed. She didn't love him the way she should. He needed to move on, all three of us did. I was tougher than Steel. I'd handled this thing far longer. "I have two more hours here. Then I'll go looking for him," I promised.

Dallas scowled like that was stupid. "He needs to go get laid."

"Tell Momma I'll find him. Don't worry about it. He doesn't need your sarcastic comments. Not right now, anyway."

"He's sure as fuck not gonna want to see you, either. We all know she broke up with him because she's still hung up on you."

No point in saying that wasn't true, "I might be exactly who he needs to see right now."

"Whatever. I'm heading to Jack's. I need a beer. This is too much fucking drama. It's like I got a bunch of goddamned sisters."

"Jack won't give you a beer. You're seventeen. But call me if he shows up there." He was already going back to his truck, "Yeah," beings his lengthy response.

When I turned around, Hannah was arranging furniture nearby, and I could tell she'd been trying to listen. There was that nosey look about her. I walked back to the truck to get the rest of the swings, hoping to avoid her questions. I got three unloaded and placed where she wanted them before she cleared her throat.

"I overheard some. I couldn't help it. He was talking loudly. Do you, uh, need help finding Steel?" Overheard my ass. She'd been straining her neck to hear us talk. I replied brusquely, "No, I need to do that alone."

She busied herself with the Adirondack chairs, fucking around with the all-weather pillows, before looking back again. "I thought they were engaged."

This town talked too damn much. "She never said yes, Hannah."

"Oh," her voice was soft. Like she was disappointed. "I can't imagine a girl turning Steel down. He's such a good guy and all."

The need to defend Dixie was strong. But I fought it. Had to let it go. "Love is a fickle bitch. Can't pick and choose where your heart will lock in. If we could, life would run a helluva lot smoother. We'd all be goofy happy."

That made her silent for a while. I was done unloading and about to ask if she needed me to rearrange anything else that was too heavy for her. Instead, she put her hands on her hips, and got that look that meant she was going to offer her opinion whether I wanted it or not.

"Some people want what they can't have. Has nothing to do

with love. It's more of a way to protect themselves from really feeling something deep. You were Dixie's first love. She's built that fantasy in her head and needs to move on from it."

Yeah. She should've kept that to herself. I counted backwards from ten before meeting her gaze, "Or maybe some things aren't your business and sticking your nose where it doesn't belong speaks volumes about you."

Her cheeks immediately flushed. I'd driven my point home and I knew I had been harsh. I wasn't a mean guy, I controlled my temper most of the time, but I couldn't stop myself on this occasion. Bray would've lit her ass on fire and left her in scalding tears. His temper could burn down a whole damn forest. But I had gone too far.

"This isn't easy. We're dealing with it the best we can. Having others who don't know the whole story give their opinions is, well, it's unkind, Hannah. There's so much shit you don't know." I was trying to ease the sting of my words and realized that I might have only made it worse.

She nodded. "Of course. You're right. I shouldn't have said anything. I don't have a filter on my mouth. My momma has always said that." She looked forlorn and I hated myself for making her feel that way.

The fact she owned up to her actions made me respect her a little more. Hannah wasn't a bad person. "We all say shit we wish we could take back, Hannah," I replied, offering her a small smile.

She smiled back. "Thanks," she returned, her cheeks still pink.

"I can appreciate it when someone knows they've messed up and owns up to it. I don't always do that myself. Not many people do."

Her soft laughter was attractive and genuine. "I have a very blunt mother. She takes no shit, and I guess it's helped me in my life, without me even knowing it."

"I figure you'd be the same either way. My momma shuts us down fast, no punches held, but not all my brothers have learned much from that. Some did, others didn't."

Hannah smirked, "I'd say you and Bray, for one, are nothing alike. I remember him from high school."

I gave her a nod and said, "None of us are like Bray, he's different from us all. Dallas, however, is running a close second on the smartass scale the older he gets."

"Bray looks hot while he's being nasty. I'm sure that helps with all the girls he goes out with."

"Like a charm," I assured her while smiling.

She laughed again. It was pleasantly appealing. Not annoying or grating for once. Hannah would make it just fine in this world. Getting to know her was nice. I could admit she was attractive and I liked more than just her looks. But my heart was not in it. When I left here today, I wouldn't think of her again until I returned to work tomorrow. Her face wouldn't stay in my mind, her smile would fade ever so quickly. Only one face always stayed with me, even when I prayed to God for some reprieve.

chapter
TWENTY-FIVE

Dixie Monroe

WORK WENT ON and on. All day I'd thought about this morning's encounter with Steel. With relief also came sadness. He'd looked at me with such hate. That was hard to accept because I didn't want him to hate me. Steel was special to me, but I understood his reaction. I didn't want him to regret the moments we'd spent together, but wanting Steel to remember me fondly was selfish of me. If he needed to hate me, then I had to accept it. I would hate me, too.

I finished cleaning up the salon and wiping down the tanning beds, which was the part of my job that I hated the most. When it was ready for reopening tomorrow, I locked up and stepped outside, coming face to face with a very drunk Steel leaning against my Jeep.

"You're either stupid or just a bitch. I can't figure it out." Steel slurred as I slowly approached him. I stated the obvious, "You're drunk." He cackled loudly, responding as if it were a mystery, "Oh, she's a sharp one, folks. Guess she's not stupid after all. Just a bitch. A mean ol' bitch."

It stung hearing Steel call me a bitch, but he was drunk and hurting, so I couldn't let it get to me. Instead, I tried to be sensible, "Get in the Jeep. I'll drive you home."

He gave me an incredulous look. "You think I'd get in that Jeep with you? Shit, girl, maybe you *are* stupid. I want nothing to do with you. Nothing! You hear that, Dixie Monroe? N-O-T-H-I-N-G!"

I could have pointed out that he was here to see me. That I hadn't gone after him. But I was dealing with a drunk man. I saw no point in arguing with him. "You can't drive like this."

He pushed off from my Jeep, held his arms wide, then revolved in a dizzying circle, spinning while flapping his arms a little. "Do you see my motherfucking truck? Do you? No, you don't. How you reckon I'm gonna drive it if it aint't here?"

Steel was right. No evidence of a truck. "So you're just walking around drunk?"

"Ain'tyourproblemwhatthefuckIdo," he snarled, but the way his words ran together, it didn't sound as angry as he hoped.

"Steel, you're here at my Jeep. I must wonder why? If I'm a stupid bitch . . ." I was not going to reason with a drunk man. I should text Brent and have him come get Steel. Bray wasn't around lately and wouldn't care if he remained on foot. And Asher . . . well, Asher was no longer someone I could contact. Yesterday, he'd made that as clear as it had ever been.

"Wanted to see if you were planning on running to Asher now that you're free of me."

"No, Steel, I'm not. Asher doesn't want me. He made that clear to me. I broke it off with you because you deserve to be loved by someone who is not me. With their whole heart, and not only half of one."

He released a nasty laugh. "Yeah. Fuck that. I don't want anything to do with love. I'm over it. I can drink and fuck my way through life. Sounds a helluva lot more fun than dating you."

I tried to hide the humiliation he made me feel with his words because Steel had more substance than that. He was kind and could love someone for life. Steel could give a woman a home and a family. I knew that. It had been one of the reasons why letting him go had been so hard. But that woman should be able to offer the same in return. I'd never been able to do that with him. His brother always stood between us and would've probably stayed there forever.

"You're meant for more than bars and one-night stands."

He stared off down the road as the cars whizzed by, "I thought so, too, but you know what, Dix, I think I'll like bars and a different woman every night just fine. That actually sounds good to me."

I guessed all men needed to be a little reckless before they finally settled down. This might have been Steel's time to have a taste of that life. But I knew it wouldn't make him happy. At least not forever. Daddy always said a man sowed his wild oats before he realized that the love of one woman was all he needed to thrive. When I'd been with Asher and thought we'd always be together, Daddy would warn me outright, "Don't be planning a wedding and babies, Dixie. That boy has wild oats to sow before he's ready for that. He goes out and comes back to you in the end, then it's a love you can trust. You need to date other men, too. Might be more to life than Asher Sutton."

I hated hearing him tell me that. I would roll my eyes and ignore it. I couldn't stand the idea of Asher being with anyone else. But that was when I thought fairytales came true, when I believed Asher was my future. My focus then returned to Steel, "Then I guess you can go see if that's the life you want. It's not my place to tell you what is right for you. You're a grown man."

He turned to me, straightening his torso. "I just might thank you one day. For breaking my fuckin' heart."

I had nothing to say to that. He began walking toward the town center. Or rather, swaying toward it. I considered following him, calling Dallas maybe to yank Steel from the street, when Asher's blue truck suddenly emerged from around the corner. The Sutton boys always took care of their own. I was no longer needed so I climbed in my Jeep and quickly drove away. Asher didn't want to see me. Steel even less. He'd said what he couldn't say sober.

I also felt a little better. This morning left me raw, the wound remaining wide open, but Steel's words made sure that it would begin to heal. Steel had been an important part of my life for a year. We'd become a couple. And I wanted us to work, until Asher came back. Now I knew that had been a lie all along. Steel would now be a part of my past, and maybe one day I could remember this and not feel sad about it. But that'd be a while from now.

Leaving this town was my only option. I had to make a new life somewhere else. I didn't want to leave my parents. I hadn't wanted to leave Scarlet either, but now she'd left me. I liked this place, I loved my home, but my life here had always been inter-twined with the Sutton boys.

A new town with new friends and a new independence would help me get on with my life. I'd tell Daddy tonight I was ready to commit to Clemson in the fall. He could pay the tuition and I'd start making plans to leave Malroy in August. My chest felt heavy from knowing I had to leave. Even though Asher would be leaving soon and finishing his last year at Florida, this town was still my connection to him. It was the place where he'd been mine.

I looked in the rearview mirror as I came to a stop at the red light. Asher was outside his truck talking to Steel who was now more animated and yelling at Asher, while Asher remained calm and relaxed. Right now, they had to be both wishing they'd never met me. Dixie Monroe had been nothing but a problem. But soon I'd be gone and they'd be rid of me for good.

chapter
TWENTY-SIX

Asher Sutton

THIS WASN'T OVER with Steel. He'd cursed me, drunkenly ranted, and then asked for Brent to come get him. I left him there with him. Brent was probably who he needed right now. They both were hurting. They both needed to drink and forget. They could drown their sorrows together. Hopefully, they wouldn't both wake up next to women they didn't know. But then maybe that was what they needed after all. As long as they stayed away from the married ones. Bray was infamous for messing around with married women he didn't realize were married. It was a miracle he hadn't been shot yet. Brent and Steel were hurting, but they were both more cautious than Bray.

I didn't want to go home and talk about Steel. He could tell them what he wanted when he was sober enough. What I needed right now was silence and my thoughts, but I knew I wouldn't find any peace. As I turned my truck onto the dirt road that led to the lake connecting our land to the Monroe's working farm, one that no one used unless Luke was fishing. At least not anymore.

My brothers and I used to swim and fish there as kids, but those days were long gone.

It had also been the spot where I'd taken Dixie's innocence. She'd told me she loved me along that grassy bank. I'd told her I loved her, too, holding her naked body snugly against mine for the very first time. Most would say any teenage boy would declare love when he had a naked female in his arms. But I knew this moment had been special. It had been honest and real. I'd known I loved her before that moment. It had just fallen from my lips as emotions washed over me like a tidal wave. She hadn't been my first, but she was my one.

I turned off my truck lights and sat there in the dark watching the moonlight dance across the water. Dad taught us to swim here. There were nights when I was away that I'd close my eyes and think of just sitting here. Recalling good days made me less homesick, but it also kept breaking my heart.

All of a sudden, movement in the corner of my eye caught my attention. I turned to see Dixie standing several feet away. She'd been sitting. I hadn't noticed. But she was leaving now. I should let her go. It was best for both of us. The right thing to do. But I couldn't. Not here and not right now. Not when some of my best memories came from this place. Here, I felt weak, my soul longing for what it couldn't have. I got out of my truck and walked to her. She stopped, didn't move, her gaze locked on me. The moonshine seemed to draw a bright halo around her, as if she didn't belong to the night.

"You come here often?" I asked. It was something I wondered about often. We had so many memories here. Did Dixie think of me when she came to the lake?

"Yes, sometimes . . . some times more than others."

She didn't have to explain that to me. After this morning with Steel, I imagined she needed to be alone, much like I did now.

"You did the right thing," I told her.

"I know," she replied, not needing my approval. "But it was the hardest thing to do."

"I wasn't being condescending. If you're out here worried about the shape you found him in earlier, drunk in the middle of town . . . he'll be okay."

She gazed back to the water, her eyes no longer on mine. "He hates me now, maybe he always will, but he said today he might thank me in the future. I don't think he meant it, but I'll hope and pray that's the case. Have to hold on to that."

Steel told me I was a selfish bastard and that he wished I would've stayed gone. He didn't want my opinion or any other moral horseshit. He said that Dixie was free now, and that I might as well go take her since that's what I'd wanted all along. I'd called Brent and let him take over. Steel was drunk, and sober or drunk, he didn't want me there.

"I'm leaving," she said, her eyes back on me, a determined gleam in them. "In August, I'm going to Clemson."

She was starting over. Getting away. That would be good for her. She'd make new friends and there would be other guys. She might even fall in love again. My heart felt like someone was squeezing it by hand at the mere idea of her loving someone else. But I had to let her go. "You'll like it there. Beautiful campus. It was one of the colleges I visited."

"I can start a new life," she said, nodding firmly, with determination in her voice. A life where I was no longer in it, unable to hurt her anymore.

We make certain choices in life because we have to. Others are made on a whim. And the rest, if we're fortunate enough, we think those through, taking our time to decide. I'm not sure which one of these scenarios made me close the distance between us, bring our bodies a breath away from one another, and cup her face in my hands. That face I'd never forget. The one I saw every night when I closed my eyes and stayed with me throughout the day. I thought of nothing else as I lowered my mouth to hers, capturing it with a kiss. I'd longed for this moment for what seemed like forever. I wanted her in my arms again, her body pressed against mine like this, and with a desperate moan, our kiss quickly escalated to a burning frenzy.

Her hands slid under my shirt, soft palms caressing my skin. I could hear my own voice in my head telling myself this had to stop, but no part of my body was listening. I couldn't force myself to do it even if I wanted to. She was leaving, moving on and I'd soon become a memory for her. That was all I knew. Maybe this was desperation, a futile echo of two people who'd loved each other deeply and were forced to let it all go. Nothing mattered to me in this moment—the past, present or future—because right now, with the moonlight playing on her face, a heavenly host surrounding this place where we'd spent so many carefree nights in the arms of the other, there was nothing but Dixie and me. If I had to choose a long life or this one last embrace with her, I'd choose this moment time and time again.

chapter
TWENTY-SEVEN

Dixie Monroe

THE ACHE I felt for Asher to touch more of me battled with the trembling from being in his arms again. I couldn't get close enough. His hands moved down my arms and squeezed my waist, Asher's tongue sliding over mine as every nerve in my body came alive. My hands gripped his back, desperate to get closer and make sure there wasn't any space between us, not an inch.

Asher grabbed my bottom and jerked me up against him. His hardness pressed into my stomach. I could feel the throb of his erection, my panties dampening even more. He lifted me gently, up and down, his pelvis rubbing against me. Asher's fingers bit into the flesh where my shorts had ridden up. I made noises I didn't know I was making, moving a hand to the front of his jeans to feel his bulge in my hand, the thickness of him in my palm causing him to lower me and my feet to touch the ground again. Terrified that this was over, that whatever control he had lost had come back, I began to open my mouth. But before I could say anything, Asher grabbed my shirt and ripped it over my head, his dark, hungry gaze locked on every inch of my body. "Take off your shorts," he demanded, discarding his own shirt, and already working the buttons of his jeans.

He watched me as I lowered my shorts. They fell on the grass beneath our feet, his eyes following their descent. "Panties, too," he ordered and I quickly tugged them to the ground. We stood there naked, Asher's eyes devouring my flesh.

I wanted his hands on me, his mouth, his body inside mine. "Asher," I began to plead.

"I want to kiss and lick every inch of your body. I want to take all night with you. But I need to be inside you, Dixie, right now," he said before I could add anything else.

I stepped closer to him and placed a hand on his chest. Tilting back my head, I stared into his eyes. I was no longer the same girl he once held and loved in this very place. I was older, stronger. I wanted everything from him, and I was not afraid to ask. "Fuck me, Asher," I said.

His eyes blazed, his hand firmly grabbing my hair, but with enough gentleness not to hurt me. "You want me to fuck you?" he asked, the heat in his eyes turning into molten fire.

"I want to still feel you in me tomorrow. I want each step I take to remind me that you were inside me."

"Jesus," he hoarsely whispered. He then spun me around by a handful of my hair, his other palm landing firmly on my butt, the sudden smack ringing through the air. I squealed from the shock and pleasure. "You like that?" he asked, doing it again.

"Yes," I replied breathlessly.

His hand kept smacking my butt, each slap stinging more than the one before it, my thighs beginning to feel the wetness between them. When he stopped, he put a knee between my legs and aggressively pushed them apart. His fingers searched for my wetness, a single digit climbing to the pulse of my clit. I cried out, my body bucking. He twisted, then pinched the quivering bundle of nerves, growling in my ear, "You're soaking wet from your spanking. You like it when I play rough."

"Yes," I panted, "I like it all."

Trapped in his arms, we moved us to his truck. He jerked open the passenger door and all but threw me on the worn seat, before covering me and opening my legs, both his hands prying them apart. I was desperate to have him inside me. I wanted anything he could give me. I'd let him do whatever he wanted.

"Tell me to fuck you again," he said, his eyes lifting to mine, their color even darker now.

"Fuck me," I replied without hesitation.

With one hard move, he pushed his length deep inside me. We both cried out as I clawed at his back, needing him to stay there. "God, that's tight," he breathed.

"I want to be sore tomorrow," I said again.

"This pussy is mine. And by the time I'm done with this pussy, you'll remember me for days."

He gently slid from my body until the tip was almost freed, before he pounded into me again. He grabbed my hair and tilted my head back, our eyes locked on each other. With each plunge and firm rock of his hips, we remained unable to look away, needing that closeness.

"This face," he said as he slammed into me, "always this face. It's all I see."

Tears stung my eyes. There was so much he was saying in just those few unguarded words.

"Is this what you wanted?" he asked as he brought my body closer to its release. "Am I fucking you hard enough?"

"Yes," my breaths were shallow, my orgasm so close it was hard to keep my eyes from closing in ecstasy.

"You're so goddamn wet. Turns you on, doesn't it, to be spanked and fucked this hard?"

"Just by you," was all I knew how to say.

He growled, satisfaction rumbling deep in his chest, and then began moving faster, his breaths quick and heavy. "I want to fuck you forever. Be right here inside you until the earth stands still. Nothing is as good as this."

I clawed at his arms, the first tremors of my orgasm taking hold. Moving in like a warm tide inside me. My mouth fell open in a cry, but my eyes stayed on him. I wanted Asher to see what he did for me, how being with him was the only pleasure I ever wanted. As I felt apart in his arms, shuddering and chanting his name, my knees pressed into his ribs, arching higher and higher to feel him as deeply as I could. Asher then freed his own release, bathing my thighs and stomach. He didn't look away, groaning my name through the shudders that caused his body to jerk.

I sat up and wrapped my arms around his waist. He'd regret this now. I knew him well enough to expect that. Before he could do that, I needed him to hold me one last time. His arms enveloped my frame and we stayed like that longer than I'd hoped. And when he finally pulled back, I didn't need to look into his eyes to know it was all over.

"I've never felt that connected to anyone. Never will," he said, his honesty surprising me. "I can't . . . not now . . . not with Steel the way he is. Dixie, there can't be more than this."

I replying tenderly, "I know."

He closed his eyes and rested his forehead on mine, "I love you, Dixie Monroe."

This was when I should have told him the same. But I'd already done that, and it'd changed nothing between us. I said instead, "I come here most nights."

He stilled. I waited as he thought that through. He then

replied, "Not sure I can resist that."

"Good. I'm glad you can't."

I wanted more of this. If it was all we could have, I was okay with that. My body was still humming from the pleasure, the addictive experience of having sex with Asher feeling like a pain killing narcotic.

He then added, "If we do that, I'm afraid I won't know how to stop."

"Good. I'm glad you can't resist me," I teased.

He laughed, his arms tightening around me. "I'd have probably cracked before now if you'd told me to fuck you like that. My dick has never been that hard. The sound of your sweet voice asking me that . . . it's a damn miracle I didn't throw you on the grass and gone at it right there like an animal."

"Next time, maybe try that. I'll even get on all fours for you." I knew I was taunting him. But the image of him behind me made my tender spots begin to tingle again.

"Dix, don't say shit like that after the pounding I just gave you. You're gonna be sore and all I can think about is doing it over and over."

I wanted him to think about me all day tomorrow. To be as crazed with lust as I would be by the time he got here. I let my hands fall as I sat back, "You're right. I need to get home."

He sighed, got out of the truck, before reaching for my hand to help me out. His gaze shifted to my body where he'd released all over me, while my eyes traveled to his penis which was once again hard and erect.

"I'll clean you up," he said, finding his shirt where he'd tossed it in the grass. I stood and let him wipe me down, knowing he wanted more. I was leaving Asher Sutton wanting me.

"Get dressed," he said, his tone sharp. I turned away before he caught me smiling. I took my time, looking over my shoulder, always finding him watching me.

"I'll see you later," I told him, heading for the path that wound up to my house.

"That's it? Not even a goodnight kiss?"

I stopped and flashed Asher a big teasing grin, "If there's a kiss goodnight, I'll most likely beg you to fuck me from behind."

He ran his hand through his hair and exhaled. Blew a long breath into the darkness, "Dixie Monroe, you're gonna kill me."

"Night, Asher," was all I said. I hurried along the path, letting myself fully absorb the reality of what we'd decided to do. What we had was no longer a fairytale. It would end and I'd be destroyed once more. But for now, Asher was mine. A small part of him belonged to me again. A part I could feel and touch, and that had to be enough.

chapter
TWENTY-EIGHT

Asher Sutton

I WASN'T SURE if, in the light of day, I'd end up regretting last night with Dixie. I knew Steel would be hurt if he found out. After yesterday and the way he'd yelled at me, I knew he'd be furious. It would most probably go to fists, with me just blocking his punches. I couldn't hit Steel, I wouldn't hurt him that way, too. Too much pain had been shared between the three of us already.

It was different yet the same with Bray, Brent and Scarlet. They had all hurt each other because what one of them had with her was stronger than what the other could ever have. They'd lied. They'd cheated. We hadn't done that to one another, only our hearts had.

I'd been selfless for years, ever since I found those damn letters. I'd made sure to protect everyone while I broke into a million pieces. That was over. The truth was out. Dixie had ended it with Steel. Why did I have to keep pushing her away? How was that fair to anybody? I hadn't dropped her and then decided I wanted her back just because my brother was with her. Hell, Steel hadn't even asked me how I felt about him dating Dixie. He kept it from me for a year. He'd not once considered how I felt. And when the truth finally came out, he didn't even care about how it affected me. He was only worried about himself and his relationship with Dixie. I would've never fucking done the same to him. We were brothers, but we were all so different.

Since dad had died, I'd been the one to make sure the others were okay. They relied on me, expected me to be there for them, but now, we were all fucking grown men. It was my turn to make a decision that would put my happiness first. I couldn't imagine my life without Dixie in it. Even when I'd tried, her face had always been there, following me into my dreams. We'd lost three years, both been hurt and scarred, but maybe we could find a way to heal together.

Dixie deserved more from me. She wanted me to fight for her, to choose her over others, something I didn't understand at first, but now I did more than ever before. I loved my brothers, but they weren't little boys anymore. I didn't always have to put their needs and wants first—we were all adults now, or almost.

Steel was hurting and I had to give him time. Once his anger had run its course and he was ready to listen, I'd talk to him about Dixie, which was more than he'd done for me. If he'd asked me beforehand, I'd have never allowed him to start a relationship with her only because of the letters, not because I did not want them to be happy. But now, things had changed and the happiness of the only woman I'd ever loved was at stake. It was time for me to put Dixie first.

As I exited the attic and walked down the hall, I heard Bray and Dallas laughing in the kitchen. I hadn't expected Bray to be up, much less laughing. He'd stayed away for days, kept his distance, but now he seemed to be acting normal again. He hadn't faced Brent yet, though. We all knew that was coming. We'd all been waiting. I doubted Brent or Steel had made it home already. If they had, they'd still be hungover in bed until Momma banged a pot with a spoon in their room to wake them up. Or a glass of ice water would be thrown in their faces like she'd done so many times before.

"Y'all sure are in good moods this early," I said, heading straight for the coffee on the counter. I didn't want to make a big deal of Bray's being out of his room.

"Norton adopted a wild mustang. You should see that thing twist and buck. It's feral. Crazy as hell." Dallas replied, as if this was a good reason to be so happy in the morning.

Bray spoke then. "They're gonna break him. Attempt to break him. But I'll believe it when I see it. I already told Norton I ain't getting on the thing. That bastard will put your dick in the dirt."

I figured that was a sound decision. "Reckon it'd be dumb to try. Never seen a wild mustang, but I hear they can be dangerous. Not meant for joy riding."

Dallas leaned back in his chair. Tucking a strand of dark hair behind his left ear, he said, "I ain't scared of no bronco."

"That's 'cause you're still a stupid little shit," Bray replied with a smirk.

"I'm bigger than you," he shot back.

"You're bigger than all of us," I added. "But that bronco is larger than you, though apparently not your ego."

His grin grew, ignoring the second part of what I said. "Yeah. Ain't that a bitch. Momma also loves me best."

Bray rolled his eyes, replying, "You're the baby. Poor woman ain't got no choice."

Dallas wasn't upset about that at all. Shrugging, he unfolded his frame to stand, reaching for the cowboy hat on the chair beside him. "And I'm the handsomest."

"Then why do they all want to suck my dick?" Bray added.

Dallas barked with laughter. "Damn, it's good to have you back."

I had to agree with him. The darkness in his eyes told me he wasn't completely back. But I'd watch him closely until he was.

"You working today?" Bray asked me.

"Yeah, I am," I replied.

"When are you heading back to Florida? Don't y'all have to start workouts and practice soon?"

I wasn't sure I was going back. I didn't want to say that yet. Momma would be disappointed if I didn't go back, get my diploma, so I said, "Next month we'll begin."

Dallas took a long swig from the gallon of milk, then looked at me. "You really gonna stay that long?"

"I need to make sure Momma is taking her medicine regularly."

Bray snorted. "And that Dixie is okay. Don't deny it. You're afraid to leave until you're sure she's fine."

I wasn't going to deny it. "That's true," I replied honestly.

Dallas was staring at me. I could see the surprise in his expression, but I didn't comment any further. Momma came walking in the door with a basket of eggs on her arm. "If you just drank directly from that gallon of milk, I'm gonna tan your hide."

Dallas shook his head, looking all innocent. "No, Momma, I was just getting it out to pour me a glass."

"After he took a long swig, that is," Bray offered, taking the eggs from momma.

Dallas glared at Bray who couldn't care less.

"Don't none of us want your backwash, boy," Momma scolded, her frown remaining in place as she went to the stove to get the lard and flour, getting everything ready to start preparing breakfast.

"That heifer's gonna have her baby this week. She's got the

look. It's about time. I was sure she'd have that calf in May. Need to move her to the small ring," she said. That was meant for all, but Bray nodded.

"Yeah, I noticed. I'll get Dallas out there with me and we'll take care of it."

Momma stopped and put her hand on Bray's cheek. "You good? Worried me sick. Ain't no girl worth that."

He nodded but his eyes betrayed him. She seemed appeased so she dropped her hand to get back to cooking.

"Neither of them other two came home last night. This ain't a boarding house. If they aren't here in the next hour, they'll be sleeping with that heifer for a week."

Dallas looked at me apologetically. "Dixie broke up with Steel. He's struggling. Brent stayed with him."

Momma stopped and turned to me. She didn't say anything at first. I was ready to defend myself. It wasn't fair that everyone blamed me for what Steel was going through.

She just said, "Guess that was coming. Good thing. She didn't love him right."

That's all she said. We went on to discuss what needed to be done on the farm until we ate and then left for work.

Just as I was walking out the door, she called my name. She'd waited until the other two were gone. "Keep an eye on him. He ain't right just yet."

I knew who she meant, so I nodded. "Yes, ma'am. I will."

chapter
TWENTY-NINE

Dixie Monroe

THE CLOCK ON the wall finally said it was lunch time. At noon, the salon closed for an hour. Everyone was free to spend their break as they pleased. The other employees usually used the tanning beds during this time or styled each other's hair. I occasionally got a wash and cut, but most of the time, I just read a book and ate a sandwich.

Today, however, I had other plans. I had decided the front desk needed a little sprucing up. A nice pot of flowers would do and I knew just where to get them. This was not what Asher and I had agreed on last night, but I wanted to see him. Maybe say hello. It wasn't like I was taking him lunch and making a scene for the town to talk about.

I called out to let them know I was leaving for my break and then headed out the door, making sure I flipped the sign on the door before I locked it up. This was the only salon in Malroy and it always closed for lunch. Customers expected it. But we still turned that sign around in case anyone forgot.

For the first time in three years, I had opened my eyes that morning and a smile had spread across my face. A real one. It was so big, it had hurt my cheeks and I'd loved every second of it. That feeling of joy, excitement, hope were all new to me now. It was a wonder I'd even gone to sleep last night. I couldn't have dreamed up a better night if I'd tried. When I'd been younger, I had imagined something like that daily. But over time it began to hurt too much to even think about it, so I'd forced myself to think of other things just to stop the pain and tears as I closed my eyes at night.

Those tears were a part of the person I'd become now, but I wouldn't miss them or the hollowness inside my chest. Asher hadn't promised me anything, but what he'd said was all I needed to hear for now. He loved me. He wanted to meet me there again tonight. And then again the next night.

I hurried down the street. Denver's Feed and Seed was only half a mile from the salon and walking there was faster than driving because there were three stop lights between the two stores.

The wooden furniture that I was sure everyone in this town owned in some shape or form in their backyard and on their porches, was displayed out front. Bright yellow sunflowers decorated the space and I had to admit even I wanted to go sit down and enjoy some lemonade. It was very welcoming. I wondered if Asher had unloaded all that. Probably had. That just made me smile even more. I didn't care at all about how goofy I must've looked grinning all alone while walking down the sidewalk.

Turning onto the gravel parking lot, I scanned the flowers on display for something affordable since I was buying these out of my own pocket. As I looked, my eyes also searched around for any signs of Asher. I didn't want to be obvious, but I knew he'd know immediately why I was here.

I made my way to the side of the building where the store's

entrance was. Just as I stepped into the shade of the overhang, I heard a female voice that made me stop in my tracks.

"Time to eat, Asher. I got you the roast beef with that dark sauce you like to dip it in. I ate a few of your fries, though." The voice belonged to Hannah and it was flirty. It also appeared to be very familiar with what Asher liked. I didn't know if I should continue walking in their direction.

"Did you get me a sweet tea?" he asked and I saw him then walking in from the back. His sleeveless undershirt was dirty and clung to his sweaty skin. He was wearing his cowboy hat and it shaded his eyes. I couldn't see his face, but his tone was friendly. And he seemed pleased.

"Of course. Oh, hi, Dixie, can I help you with something?" Hannah asked and I shifted my focus to her. She was giving me a fake smile. It was too bright and it didn't meet her eyes.

"I, uh, no, I'm just, I," I stopped stuttering and pointed to a wall of hoes and shovels, then hurried toward them.

"Dixie," Asher's voice called after me. I was not turning around. She'd caught me off guard. I hadn't been prepared to speak yet. Not as I was still processing what I had witnessed.

Maybe they were just friends. He said before they were friends and I believed him. But the way she had talked to him, the tone in her voice . . . it said something else.

"Dixie, wait," he was closing in on me. I could start running, but then I'd look ridiculous and draw even more attention to myself. That would, of course, make Asher and I the topic of everyone's dinner conversation tonight. Including my own family's. Wincing, I stopped walking and just waited on him to reach me.

His fingers wrapped around my upper arm and I let him turn me around. "Why did you walk off?" He looked completely confused.

"I don't know," I lied. I knew I was overreacting.

He frowned and looked around. "Come out back to my truck."

I felt eyes on me. I was almost positive they belonged to Hannah, but I didn't check. I didn't care. I only cared about being alone with Asher.

"Okay," I acquiesced and let him lead me to the back. Once we were around the storage bins, his truck came into view. When we were on the far side of the truck, hidden from view, he backed me up against it and placed his hands on either side of me. His palms sat flat on the door behind me. "Tell me what just happened."

Sighing, I closed my eyes because this was embarrassing. "I came to get flowers for the salon in hopes of seeing you. Then I heard you and Hannah talking. Y'all were friendly. She was being flirty with you."

Asher put a finger under my chin and tilted my head back. "Open your eyes, Dix," he sounded amused. I slowly opened them and then blinked against the sun.

"Hannah is my friend. We work together."

I nodded.

He just smirked and pressed a kiss to my lips. "I like you jealous. I have to admit it."

"I don't," I pouted.

He laughed, but then dropped his hands from the truck behind me and stood back up straight. "I've got to eat lunch, you've got to get flowers, and if I stay back here with you any longer, I'll start kissing you the way I want to. We can't do that just yet. Not in public."

Because of Steel.

"Okay," I replied, wishing things were different. But I understood.

"Come on," he said with a gentle tug of my hand, walking us back around the truck. I wasn't embarrassed anymore, so when my eyes found Hannah looking at us, I smiled. I didn't care what she thought of me. I had acted silly and if she wanted to think I was nuts, I couldn't blame her.

"I'd share half my sandwich with you if it wouldn't make people talk," he said.

"I'll eat back at the salon."

"I won't enjoy my lunch company. I promise."

I laughed at that. He quickly squeezed my hand, then moved away.

It wasn't until I lifted my eyes to start looking for flowers that I saw him. Steel. He was standing just outside his truck watching us. His angry glare caused my breath to hitch, making Asher follow my gaze. He tensed and immediately put distance between us.

"Come on, you. Time to eat. Thanks for helping Dixie with that. I had no idea where to find it," Hannah said brightly as she walked in between us and wrapped her arms around Asher's arm.

"Wha—" Asher started to say, but then nodded. "Yeah. No problem."

Hannah was saving him from Steel. I understood that, but it still didn't feel good to see her cuddling up against him. "Oh, hey, Steel!" she called out waving and walking Asher away from me. She glanced back at me. "Just take what you need to the front. Nora will check you out. We're taking our lunch now." There was a challenge in her gaze as she looked at me. Then she gave me a slow smile, went up on her toes and pressed a kiss to Asher's face. "He's just the sweetest."

I waited to see him push her away. To tell her to stop. To question why she thought she could do that. But he did none of those things. He let her continue to cling to him. I didn't want to watch anymore. My stomach felt sick as I walked away, back toward the street. Away from Steel, away from Asher, and away from Hannah. I didn't want to pretend anymore. I had pretended for years. Pretended that I was okay. That I wasn't hurting every single day. That I wasn't lost. I was done with it all.

Last night, I'd allowed myself to hope that maybe sometime soon, Asher would want to fight for me, too. That after the sex, he'd want more. He'd want back what we had taken from us. But what I'd just witnessed hadn't been fighting. That had been acting. That had been just one more lie to add to the growing pile between us all.

chapter
THIRTY

Asher Sutton

"**T**HAT FUCKING QUICK?**"** Steel asked as he continued glaring at me like he hated the sight of me. I wanted to see if Dixie was gone, but I knew not to look in her direction. Steel would go crazy and I didn't want him doing that here.

"Not what you think it is," I told him.

"She just came by needing help with some flowers for the salon. I had Asher show her the newest stock out back that we haven't displayed yet. That's all, Steel," Hannah offered cheerfully. She was a good actress, her easy-going tone convincing and confident, and the way she stayed attached to my arm suggested that something was happening between us.

Steel looked at Hannah, then back to me. "You fucking her?" he asked. I wasn't sure if he meant Hannah or Dixie.

"Steel," I started to correct him, because Mr. Horn, the nearly eighty-years-old pastor at the Baptist church, had just heard him cuss while he shopped for gardening gloves for his wife. But

Hannah interrupted me.

"Our sex life isn't your business, Steel. Never will be, either."

Hannah and I would never have a sex life. I didn't correct her, though. I'd do that later after Steel had left. If this was just a grand act to appease him, then I was thankful for it. Bit if she thought it was the beginning of anything more between us, I needed to clarify to her that it wasn't.

He continued to study us.

"You been home? Momma is worried."

He shrugged "She's pissed as hell. Not worried."

"That, too," I agreed.

More silence filled the space between us.

"She only loved you. Never loved me," he said before walking away. He sounded defeated. I wanted to tell him that he meant something to her. That he'd been important to her. Instead, I just let him go, hating myself for putting that pain in his eyes.

"She's really messed with his head," Hannah said in a whisper.

If the past wasn't what it was, if things hadn't happened the way they did, if a lie hadn't kept us apart, I'd agree with her. But Dixie was as much a victim as he was. We all were.

"She never meant to," I told her.

"You sure?" Hannah asked.

I moved away from her and was tempted to just walk back to my truck and drive off, away from the questions. Back to the lake where nothing mattered but me and Dixie. But I couldn't do that.

"There is more to the story than you know."

She frowned. "Then tell me."

"It's not something I can share." I replied and walked away from more questions. Hannah had helped me. I appreciated it. But that didn't give her access to my personal life, past or present.

I forgot about lunch and went to hauling the ten-pound bags of fertilizer from the trailer to the display area. The heat and sweat quickly replaced my thoughts of Dixie and Steel.

It was ten minutes before quitting time when Hannah walked back to my truck. Her sunglasses were perched on the top of her head and her purse was slung over her shoulder. She was leaving.

"You don't realize what you're missing being hung up on the past," she said. It sounded like she'd been working on that line for hours.

I pulled my work gloves off and then lifted my hat from my head to let the breeze hit my forehead, before I responded, "Until you know what Dixie and I have, don't jump to conclusions, Hannah."

She thought about that for a moment. Hannah didn't annoy me too much. I even liked her at times. But at this moment, I was ready to snap at her. Her tendency to judge without knowing all the facts was beginning to wear on my nerves.

"You'll crush Steel," she said matter-of-factly.

It was none of her business, but I had to defend Dixie. "He didn't consider me when he decided to date her."

"But you broke up with her."

I was done having this conversation with Hannah. My patience had worn thin.

"Again, you don't know the whole story so please stay out of it. Now, excuse me, but it's time for me to leave."

I didn't give her time to shoot more questions my way or say anything else. I didn't want to see her face again today. As much as she'd saved things earlier, she'd ruined it all by sticking her nose where it didn't belong, trying to hurt the one I loved.

While walking to my truck, Hannah called out to me, "I'm here when this blows up in your face."

I didn't need or want her to be there. But I held my anger in check and just kept walking.

When I was finally inside my truck and away from Hannah,

I breathed a sigh of relief. Tonight, I would see Dixie again. We'd meet at the lake and she would be mine there. There would be no hiding. No secrets. Just us. I could get through anything knowing that was coming. Even a dinner with my brothers and a very pissed off Steel.

He'd calm down eventually and see this was best for him. I knew I should just admit my feeling for Dixie and face the consequences, but I couldn't. Not yet. He needed some time first.

Dixie didn't deserve to be anyone's dirty little secret and not even protecting Steel justified her becoming one. I had to figure out what was best for everyone, but that would take some thought. For now, we had our lake. I had Dixie. And my thoughts were no longer just memories of better times that kept slicing me open.

Dixie Monroe had always been meant to be mine. Our connection didn't dwindle even when everything had been thrown at us to keep us apart. We'd have our future one day. I had to believe that.

chapter
THIRTY-ONE

Dixie Monroe

WHEN I WOKE up this morning, I'd had a romantic evening with Asher all planned out in my head, where I would be in his arms again and there would be no more pretending. No more half-truths. But like most things in my life, things didn't go as planned. I'd come to the lake an hour early. To think. I needed to decide if I could do this. If I could possibly set myself up for a crushing end again.

I wanted a storybook romance. One where we loved each other, put each other first, had no secrets between us. One where we were free to be ourselves. Everything we never had. Being together now filled us both with fear, guilt, regret, yet we wanted it so desperately, we were willing to pretend. For a few hours, we pretended we had everything, only to wake up to the deafening tick-tocks of a reality check.

It had taken me so long to even find the will to live after I'd lost Asher. Just laughing again had required so much effort. I didn't know whether I was willing to go through that again, or whether

I even still loved him enough to take a chance on us.

Did he love me enough to face his own family just to be with me?

All this was running through my head when his truck pulled up nearby. I didn't run to him like I used to do, eager to greet him and show him how much I was happy to see him. The urgency to be in his arms in moments like these wasn't as strong because I no longer felt certain of his love. These doubts held me back, held my whole heart back.

He parked, cut his lights, and walked over to sit down beside me. He didn't speak at first. It was as if he was reading my thoughts, assessing them in his own mind, before acting. I let him do it. What happened at his work today had opened my eyes to what I might have to endure if we ever decided to continue this in any way.

Hannah got to eat lunch with him, laugh with him, be with him in public. All the things I couldn't get. How long would it be before he got tired and wanted that too? How long would it be before he went looking for it elsewhere?

"He just needs more time," Asher finally broke the silence.

"So until then, I have to let Hannah or Amber or Emily enjoy you in ways I can't." It wasn't a question. It was a statement of truth. A painful fact.

He turned to me. "No. Of course, not. I'm not with them. I never will be with any of them. It's just you, Dix," he pleaded.

He didn't get it. He thought moments like these where no one could see us would be enough for me. "Today, you were with Hannah. She got to spend time with you. She got to laugh with you. She got to eat lunch with you for the whole world to see. All things I can't have."

His hand covered mine. "She means nothing to me. She's just a friend. Heck, she's even barely that. She's a coworker. We don't hang out after work. Today, she put up an act entirely for Steel's sake."

"No, she acted to please you. To touch you. To make you like her. And to claim you in front of me."

I sounded jealous and crazy. I knew that. But I couldn't stop the words spilling from my mouth. My heart was hurting inside my chest.

"Dix, look at me," he said as his finger slid under my chin and turned my face toward his. "It's only you and it's only ever been you. I told you that. I've told Hannah that. And after Steel's had some time to adjust, I will tell him that, too."

"What if while I'm waiting, your feelings for me change? I'd have to move on again and it almost killed me last time, Asher. I'm not sure I have the strength to—"

Asher lowered his lips to mine to silence them, pressing ever so gently. "It's always been you, Dix. Just you. There is no way I could ever stop loving you. God knows I've tried."

I let him kiss me again. I let myself trust his lips, hear every silent promise they were making. I let myself forget that he hadn't been fighting for me, that he had turned us into a dirty little secret just to protect his family. But I only allowed myself to forget for a brief moment. I knew it was time I protected myself against anyone who was not willing to put me first, regardless of how much I loved him.

I gathered enough willpower to break the kiss and put some distance between us. I didn't look at him in the eyes, knowing the love I'd find in them would break my resolve. But I needed him just one last time, I needed that connection between us, I needed to feel Asher inside me one more time, before I let him go. He had to decide all on his own after that if he was going to fight for me or not.

"Fuck me," I said while my mind was screaming to beg him

to make love to me. To love my body gently, to show me that I was not alone in this.

He ran his hand down my bare arm. "Tonight, let me take it slow."

I knew that if he took it slow, I'd break into a million pieces. I desperately wanted it, but I was too weak to have it. "Not tonight. I need you inside me. Now."

His pupils grew larger and the sweet left his eyes, replaced by raw hunger. He wanted it as much as I did. He didn't order me to get naked this time around. Instead, he did it for me, jerking my tank top off first, then pushing me back onto the grass so he could pull my shorts and panties off. "I spent a fucking hour in the shower this morning thinking about this," he growled tossing his shirt aside and unbuttoning his jeans. "How tight your pussy is, how wet it gets, how it feels when you claw my back."

I let my legs fall open and his eyes went directly to my wet opening. "Keep talking like that and I'll orgasm without you," I panted, my chest rising and falling rapidly.

"You sure you don't want me to take my time? I could eat this pussy until you're screaming for me to stop. Then fill you up nice and slow."

What woman wouldn't want that? But my heart begged me not to take it.

"Please, Asher," I pleaded.

His body came down over mine and with a firm thrust he was inside me. I screamed, curving my back and lifting my legs to wrap myself tightly around him. He started moving immediately. His arms flexed with each thrust, his breathing deep then short and shallow. He murmured words in my ear that I had to close my eyes to block out. Hearing him tell me how much he loved me and what I meant to him was splintering my heart because I felt the same way and couldn't tell him. Not before it was safe for me to do so.

When I began to tremble and cry out in release, he held me close. I let myself just inhale his scent, feel him inside me and everywhere around me, and a small tear tricked from the corner of my eye and hid in my hair. In that moment, we were as we always should have been. We were happy, connected, complete. A second tear followed when I realized we might never have this again.

chapter
THIRTY-TWO

Asher Sutton

YELLING PULLED ME out of my sleep the next morning. I was up in the attic but I could still hear the words being hurled downstairs. Jumping out of bed and grabbing a pair of sweats to quickly pull on, I ran down the stairs as quickly as I could. We'd been waiting for things to escalate between Brent and Bray and it sounded like that moment had arrived.

I came to a stop as I turned the corner and walked into the kitchen. Bray swung his angry snarl at me. "Go the fuck back upstairs. We don't need a referee," he scowled knowing well why I was here.

"The hell you don't," interjected Dallas. "Calm them the fuck down." He was looking at me now.

"Or why don't y'all let me deal with this myself? The motherfucker was screwing my girlfriend. Dixie broke up with Steel, but not because she was fucking Asher. Because Asher wouldn't do that to his own brother." Brent's tone was hard, but calm. He was angry, but he wasn't on the verge of hitting anyone.

"It ain't you we're worried about. It's the crazy ass one," Steel said looking pointedly at Bray.

"She left. She fucking left. She left us both. What the fuck does it matter now? She obviously didn't feel the same way either of us did," Bray said without the anger I expected to seep from his words. He sounded hollow. Empty. A feeling I understood all too well.

"I just want to know why? Am I asking too much, Bray? Can't you even give me a fucking reason why?" Brent was getting angrier now.

He slowly turned his gaze to his twin who simply replied, "No."

"You motherfucking asshole," Brent roared and moved fast. He was almost on top of Bray when Steel and Dallas grabbed him by the arms.

"He's already got a black eye and swollen nose because of Asher," Steel said holding him off Bray.

"Let him at me. I'll give him one shot. Then I'm fighting back."

I just watched it all unfold, not sure if this was their fight to finish. There was pain on both sides. They were closer than the rest of us. They had a bond none of us had. But what had happened with Scarlet was hard to overcome.

"You just take whatever you want, not caring about anyone but yourself, and when you end up hurting people, you use your temper as an excuse. You pitch a damn fit whenever you can't get what you want."

I was the oldest. They were waiting on me to arbitrate between them. To stop them when things got out of hand. It was what I had always done. But this was different. They were men, not boys anymore. "Let Brent go. This ain't our fight to stop.

But if you're going to hit each other, take it outside and out of Momma's kitchen."

Brent stormed past everyone and opened the screen door. "Then get your ass outside," he said shooting a challenge back at Bray.

Steel and Dallas looked at me like I'd lost my mind. I turned to them and shrugged. "It's their fight. They need this."

Bray was at the door when he put his hand on the screen and glanced back at Steel then me. "Since we're all getting our shit out and dealing with things, why don't you tell Steel about the fact you've been fucking Dixie down at the lake since she left him."

I turned just as Steel's fist met my face.

"Better take that shit outside," Bray drawled, disappearing out the door.

"Holy hell," Dallas muttered as I followed Bray outside. "Are y'all really about to just beat the shit out of each other?"

No one looked at him. No one even acknowledged his question. We all heard it but there was too much anger in the air to stop any of it now. I watched as Brent slammed into Bray and they went rolling down the grass hill behind them. Then I turned and looked at Steel. "You can have one more. Then I'm getting mine. Because I had her first. She was mine before she was yours."

Steel glared at me. "You broke her heart."

"And you know I had a good reason."

Steel advanced on me. "We never even had sex."

"Good."

That was all it took. Steel's hand connected with my jaw again and I let him. I took in two hits and then I just wrestled him until he was out of breath, evading his hits as well as I could. He put his hands on his knees and stared at the ground for several moments before tilting his head back and looking at me. "I loved her."

"I still do. Never stopped and you knew it. Just didn't care."

He winced and looked away. "Always wanted her. She was my age. Too young for you, but she only ever saw you."

"We didn't plan this. You can't plan what your heart wants."

Steel sank down and sat on the ground. He stretched his feet out in front of him and got in a relaxed position. "Fuck if I know that."

"I never touched her when you were with her."

He nodded. "I know."

I looked down the hill where grunts and hits were still filling the air. "Think we should stop them yet?" Steel asked.

"They're gonna fucking kill each other," Dallas said glaring at the two of us like we had lost our minds. "If you two are done, then help me save Brent's face before Bray bashes it in. All this over damn women. Jesus, could y'all not just find other women and stop falling for the same ones?"

"Wait until you fall in love," Steel said to him.

He shook his head. "Sure as hell won't be Scarlet or Dixie. I can abso-fuckin'-lutely promise you that."

Steel grinned and I knew we were going to be okay. Eventually. Maybe not tomorrow or next week, but one day, all this would be behind us. One day we could all be happy for each other.

"Come on, let's go stop them. Not sure they'll stop on their own," I told Steel, standing up.

"About damn time. You two take a few swings then chat it out while Brent's getting beat to death," Dallas said running down the hill.

"Get your asses up off that grass and stop that nonsense. I'm not having it. It's ridiculous and a waste of time. That girl's done run off. Get over it, the both of you," Momma's voice rang over the yard as she stood with a basket full of tomatoes from the garden.

Both of them paused.

"I mean it. Go wash the blood off," she looked our way. "All of you. Then get to work. I ain't making no breakfast for the likes of this bunch. Acting such a way as that."

Brent and Bray didn't make a move to continue.

"What about me? I didn't fight with anyone." Dallas said looking panicked over the idea of no breakfast.

"I'm sure you did something to be punished. Fix yourself some cheese toast. I got work to do."

She didn't wait to see if we did as she said. She just knew we would. Brent didn't look as bad as Dallas was sure he would. They looked equally beaten to me. Brent's anger and hurt had given him more of a fight.

Their hurt wouldn't heal any time soon. What Bray had done couldn't be forgiven easily. Brent would need a lot of time.

He looked at Bray. "This doesn't make it okay." That was all he said before walking up the hill and out to the barn to wash up.

"Fucking women," Dallas said shaking his head.

One day he'd meet one that made him change his mind.

We didn't get all washed up nor did we get ready for work.

The ambulance siren stopped us all. It was close. Too close.

chapter
THIRTY-THREE

Luke Monroe

STANDING OUTSIDE THE barn, I heard Charlotte scream-ing hysterically. I think I died a thousand deaths in that moment. The terrified sound coming from my wife was unlike anything I'd ever witnessed. The time it took for me to run from the barn to the house seemed forever although it was only seconds. My whole world was is that house. With each foot I got closer to the house, I knew I wasn't ready to face what was awaiting me inside.

Bursting through the door, I found Charlotte bent over my daughter's limp body doing CPR. For a second, my vision went blank. I quickly moved her out of the way and took over.

"Ambulance is on its way," she wailed. "She was just standing there when she suddenly went pale and collapsed. I thought she'd fainted. But her heart," Charlotte let out a loud sob. "Oh, God, please don't take our baby. Please, God, please," she begged as I continued doing chest compressions to get Dixie's heart beating again. My own seemed to have stopped. My baby girl was lifeless under my hands. No parent should ever have to experience this.

The siren came, but I didn't stop. I heard Charlotte run to the door, screaming at them to hurry. I just kept pressing on her chest, begging her heart to start beating. I wasn't letting my girl die. She was too young and so full of life. This wasn't happening.

I felt hands on my shoulders trying to move me back, but I fought against them. "No! She needs me!" I screamed.

"Luke, let them save her," Charlotte pleaded. "Please, save her!" she cried out at the EMTs who were now using a defibrillator on Dixie. Right there on our living room floor.

"It's beating," One man yelled as another moved her to a stretcher.

"Life Flight is here," another said.

I ran after them as they hurried my baby out the door and to the helicopter that had landed in my front yard.

I saw the Sutton boys running up the hill just as they were loading Dixie onto the helicopter.

"We're taking her to Memorial," a woman explained to me and hurried in behind them.

"We can give you a ride in the ambulance. It will be quicker," the man who had moved me off Dixie offered.

Charlotte was weeping uncontrollably. I turned to her only to realize my own vision was blurred from tears. What had just happened?

"Mr. and Mrs. Monroe, are you ready to leave?"

I couldn't move. My little girl was unconscious and being taken to a hospital in a helicopter. "What happened?" I asked, shaking my head in confusion.

"We don't know yet. But they will soon."

Charlotte buried herself against my chest, her sobs turning into full body shakes.

"What happened?" Asher Sutton roared from nearby, his

face void of color and the same terror running through my veins mirrored in his own eyes.

"We need to go. Get you there as soon as possible," the EMT insisted.

"They need to get to their daughter, so we're going to have to ask you all to move back," the man said addressing the Sutton boys who all stood behind Asher, looking stricken.

Climbing into the back of the ambulance, I felt like I wasn't in my body anymore. It felt like I was hovering above, watching all this unfold. This couldn't be real. This wasn't happening. I heard Asher Sutton demanding answers and pleading for some hope. I heard them give him the hospital name before the doors to the ambulance closed and the sirens started to howl.

Never had I felt so helpless.

Charlotte Monroe

I HAD JUST finished cleaning up the breakfast table when I realized that Dixie hadn't come down as early as she normally did on work days. I'd called up to her and she'd said she'd be down in a minute. When she walked into the living room, her face looked ashen and her eyes tired.

"Are you sick, sweetheart?" I had asked.

She frowned. "I think I might be. I was fine when I woke up, but as soon as I started walking around, I began to feel funny. I feel weak and I can't take really deep breaths. It's weird."

I became concerned. "I hope you've not got that flu going around. It's a nasty stomach one. You may be dehydrated. Let me get you some juice. Sit down. I'll call the salon and let them know you're not well."

She nodded. "Okay." But she didn't move. Her eyes appeared

to lose focus as she stared at me. As if they were suddenly empty.

Then she'd just collapsed right there. On the floor.

I closed my eyes as the horror of those moments replayed over and over in my head. I'd checked her pulse then and couldn't find it. If it was there, it was weak. Too weak. The screaming, calling for help, and then working to bring her back all ran together into one horrifying memory. I felt paralyzed by fear.

A loud sob startled me and I felt Luke's body shudder against mine. He wailed. The sound of pure pain. One that only a parent could feel for his child. His little girl. Another wail ripped through him and I held onto him. He'd been strong. Worked on her heart without pause. Now he was breaking apart and I wasn't whole myself. We were slowly shattering together.

"My baby," he sobbed as he held onto me. Tears streamed down my face. This was the first time I'd ever heard my husband cry. I wanted to tell him she would be okay. That she was going to be fine. But I needed someone to tell me that. She wasn't mine by blood, but she'd been mine by heart for many many years. And if she didn't make it, she'd take my heart with her, too.

chapter
THIRTY-FOUR

Asher Sutton

B RAY WAS DRIVING. I didn't remember much about getting in the truck. I heard the EMTs say her heart had stopped and that they didn't know why. That was all I knew. Nothing more. Then they drove off, leaving me only with the name of the hospital to which they took her.

This didn't seem real. It was as if I'd been stuck in a nightmare unable to wake up. The horror and fear on her parents' faces said all I needed to know.

I had to get to that hospital. She wasn't leaving me. She was too young. Healthy eighteen-year-old girls didn't need Life Flight. They'd fix this. She'd be fine. She had to be fine.

"Breathe, Ash, Breathe," Brent said as his hand touched my back. I inhaled sharply and my lungs burned. Similar to the way they did when we were kids and would compete against each other to see who could hold their breath the longest under water. I hadn't even realized I'd stopped breathing. That was the second time Brent had to remind me.

"Not much further," Bray said glancing up at me through the rearview mirror. I couldn't respond. Speaking required too much. I was doing all I could to keep it together. My cheeks were wet from silent tears. Fear, disbelief, pain, all mixed inside me, reminding me I couldn't live without Dixie.

My brothers weren't talking either. Not much, anyway. Dixie was special to all of us. She'd been in our lives as long as we could remember. Momma was on her way, too. Dallas was driving her. She was getting the people in the local churches to pray and she also packed me some things because she knew I'd stay there with Dixie. I wouldn't leave until she could. And Dixie would leave. She'd come back home with me.

"Think they'd tell us anything if we called the hospital?" Steel asked.

"Doubt it. Family only," Brent said.

I just stared out the window. We had to get there. She needed me there.

"Did the EMT say anything more, Bray?" Brent asked. Bray had talked to them more than any of us. I'd been out of my mind. I still was. I wouldn't okay until I saw her. Talked to her.

"No," he said glancing up in the rearview mirror again with a concerned look. He knew more, he just wasn't telling us.

"If you know something, then I want to know," I told him, speaking for the first time.

Bray didn't look at me this time. He remained silent.

"If you know something," I started and Steel looked at me.

"Don't. None of us know any facts. Let's just get there."

He was right. I needed facts.

It had been a helicopter. Motherfucking Life Flight. I'd only ever seen one after a car accident. When someone had almost died from the injuries. Not at someone's house. And not there to collect an eighteen-year-old.

"Get out here," Bray said pulling in front of a building. A large red sign in front of us said Emergency. We were here. "I'll park and meet y'all inside."

I didn't wait. I was out of the car and inside within seconds. I ran to the lady at the sign in sheet. "Dixie Monroe. She was brought in by Life Flight. Do you have information on her? "

The lady casually looked at her computer smacking her gum like I hadn't just said the words Life Flight. This was no big deal to her. She'd been desensitized by other people's nightmares.

"She's not in the ER," the woman said frowning. "She's admitted, though. She's in the Intensive Cardiac Care Unit."

I had no fucking idea what that meant other than she was alive. Right now, that was enough. "Where is that?"

"Go left around the large turn, then take the elevators on your right to the fifth floor. Take a left then and go straight until you see the waiting room."

Bray was inside now. The four of us headed in the direction we were told. I knew that, even without telling them to do it, that one would text Dallas and give him directions. I was always the one who kept them together, stood with them, ready to face anything and anyone. Making sure everyone was taken care of. Not now. Now, they were standing with me. By my side. Because they all knew that if something were to happen to her, I'd fall apart. She was my center.

Walking toward the waiting room, I could see Luke pacing in front of it. He ran his hand over his balding head and the tense lines of his face were obvious even from afar. Charlotte saw us first. She stood up and walked toward me, pulling me into a hug. "She's alive," she whispered in both relief and desperation. Because that didn't mean she was okay.

"What happened?"

"She just . . . collapsed. Her heart stopped. There's the doctor," she said letting me go and hurrying over to Luke who was already there in front of the man dressed in white.

"Would you like to go somewhere private?" the doctor asked.

Luke looked back at us, at me standing there. "No. This is her family," he said.

The doctor nodded. "Dixie has a rare congenital heart condition called Long QT Syndrome. Many people have no signs or symptoms until the moment their heart stops, thus ending their life. It almost always goes undetected until it's too late. Dixie was lucky. Her mother was there with her and you kept her heart pumping until the paramedics could revive her. Most aren't that lucky. I want you to understand the severity of what she's been through and that she isn't in the clear just yet. We have put her in a drug induced coma and packed her in ice to bring her temperature down. In two days, we will warm her back up and bring her out of the coma. She will be in it for about four days total. I have done this before and it's been successful. And I've done it and it hasn't been. But we will do our absolute best to bring her through this. She's a fighter. Once she's brought out of the coma, we will then fit her for an implantable cardioverter defibrillator that will regulate her heartbeat."

Her heart had stopped. Dear God, she could have died. Today. I'd have never gotten to hold her again. We wouldn't grow old together. She'd have never grown old. The idea of it rocked me. I sank down onto the closest chair and buried my head in my hands. She didn't die. She was alive. The coma they had put her in scared the fuck out of me. She had to open her eyes and look at me. She had to let me tell her we were forever. She had to let me give her everything she ever wanted, everything she deserved. It wasn't over yet. We still had a lifetime to live first.

chapter
THIRTY-FIVE

Asher Sutton

I OPENED MY eyes squinting against the sun now coming through the waiting room window. I saw Scarlet sitting across from me. She had her knees pulled up under her chin and her arms wrapped around her legs. She had no makeup and her hair was in a messy knot on top of her head, but she was still the same striking redhead that had almost torn my brothers apart. She was Dixie's best friend and I was happy she was here. I just hoped Brent and Bray weren't back anytime soon.

Sitting up, I yawned and stretched. She dropped her knees and straightened. She looked like she was ready to be told to leave, or worse.

"Someone must have known where to contact you. Dixie will be happy you're here."

My words seemed to ease her some.

"Charlotte called last night," she said.

"Good."

She was quiet for a few minutes staring down at her hands.

"I must have missed some things since it isn't Steel sleeping on those chairs."

I was the only one still here. Her parents had paid for a guest room. The rest had gone to a hotel. But I wasn't leaving. Not while she was here fighting for her life.

"She broke it up with Steel a couple of days after you left."

"I figured it was something like that." She paused, then added, "Charlotte said her heart stopped."

The screaming, the sirens, the helicopter. I could still her them in my head. I'd never forget them. I knew I'd keep re-living the horror of those moments in my nightmares.

"She's going to wake up, isn't she?" Her words were both a question and a statement, a plea stemming out of her fear.

"She'll wake up. Dixie is strong. You know that." I had to believe that.

Scarlet nodded, but then frowned. "How long do I have? When do the others get here?"

"They're all at a hotel with Momma. I expect they'll be here in an hour. I can text Steel to let me know when they're headed this way."

"Is it that bad? Do you think I need to leave?"

I didn't want her to feel like she couldn't stay, but I knew her presence here would hurt my brothers even more at a time when they were already hurting. "They've come to blows. It didn't fix things. They're not the same, Scarlet."

She hung her head and closed her eyes. "I wasn't thinking. I should have never let Brent believe I loved him." She shook her head as if to clear it and stood up. "But that's not what is import-ant now. Dixie is what's important and when she wakes up, she will need you here. Not me. I'm going to go, but I won't go far. I'll ask Charlotte to keep me updated."

This wasn't easy for her. I knew that. I would have understood had she wanted to stay. All the drama with my brothers felt less important right now.

Scarlet hadn't been gone long when my mom and brothers returned. Momma came to sit beside me and put a bag with what smelled like buttered biscuits and bacon in my lap. "Eat," she said. "Won't be as good as mine, but it'll do. You need to eat."

I didn't have an appetite, but telling her that was pointless. She'd make me eat anyway. So I did as I was told.

"Heard anything?" Brent asked, sitting down in the seat Scarlet had been in not long ago.

I thought about telling him and Bray, but decided against it. "No," I just answered.

Momma patted my leg. "I had Brent pull this condition she has up on the internet with that phone of his. I read about it. She one of the lucky ones. And she can live with this. Now that they know about it, they can keep a watch on it."

I'd done the same. I had read everything I could find on my phone about this Syndrome. The doctor hadn't been exaggerating when he said she was lucky. She'd shown no symptoms until she collapsed, and she could have easily died then had Charlotte not been there to see it and act fast.

Even once she was released, I didn't know how I would ever let her out of my sight again. My fear of something happening to her again wasn't going to go away overnight. I knew I had to deal with this.

Her mother walked into the waiting room. "They'll be taking the ice away and warming her up today. The doctor said she is responding well. He feels good about it all so far."

I felt both relieved and stressed even more. Something could go wrong. They weren't talking about that, but I knew it could. I suddenly needed some air. I felt like the whole room was closing in on me.

"I'm going for a walk," I said and headed for the door without looking back.

When I got outside the waiting room, I leaned against the wall and closed my eyes. She needed me to be strong for her. To believe she could do this. I wanted to be strong. But right now, all I wanted to do was cry. All I could think about was that I could lose her. That fear was slowly choking me.

The door behind me then opened and while I expected to see my mother walking through it, my eyes found Charlotte. I got myself together. She didn't need to see me breaking down. She was scared as it is and I didn't need to add to it.

"Sorry. My family can be too much sometimes," I said, wondering if she was needing to get away from them too.

She smiled. "They're fine. Great, really. Having all of you here means a lot."

Several of the people from their church had come by, including the pastor. They'd brought flowers and snacks. But no one had stayed overnight. Dixie's aunt was in town, as was her grandmother. They'd come yesterday and said they would be back today.

"I can't leave her."

Charlotte nodded. "And if it were you in there, she wouldn't be able to leave you either. She'd be much like you are now, doing all she could to hold herself together. The two of you," she smiled to herself before continuing. "You've been dancing around each other since you were kids. You worried you were too old, she worried you'd never see her for more than a little girl. Then when you finally come together, those letters appear and ruin it all. So many obstacles. So much pain. Yet here you are. Not leaving this hospital. That's what happens when you know you've found the one. I once told her you weren't it. That there was someone else out there for her. I wanted it to be true because I wanted her to have a chance to be happy. But I see now she knew better. You two make a whole. Knowing she found that, that she found you at such a young age, gives me hope that she will fight to open her eyes. That she will fight to live. That she will fight to come back to us."

chapter
THIRTY-SIX

Asher Sutton

THE WAITING ROOM was slowly filling up. I'd woken up here for the third morning in a row to find more and more people from Malroy arriving. The girls from the salon, Norton Knolls and his wife, Denver Watson, even Amber and Hannah, as well as faces that were familiar but I couldn't place. I kept my head down, mostly, lost in my thoughts. They'd be waking her up today. Or trying to. The doctor had said there was a chance she would go into her own coma and then we'd have to wait it out. I wanted to see her eyes. God, I wanted to hold her hand and promise her that we'd get to be all she wanted us to be. I would bust my ass to make sure the past three years became a distant memory for her.

As nice as it was that these people were here offering their support to Luke and Charlotte, I wished they'd all go away. The voices around me were grating on my nerves. I needed silence. I needed to think of all the ways I would try to make Dixie happy.

"Brent said you haven't left at all." Hannah had kept her

distance until now, but she had worked her way over to me.

I nodded. What was I supposed to say to that? Of course I hadn't fucking left.

"Can I go get you something?"

This wasn't the Feed and Seed. This wasn't a lunch break. It was the damn hospital. Did she think a sandwich would make it all better?

"No," I knew I was being rude, but I couldn't get myself to care. Dixie might never wake up and I'd be here eating a damn sandwich.

She didn't say anything after that. She just sat there beside me in silent support. But I kept thinking that Dixie wouldn't want her there beside me. I needed her to go. Talk to someone else. Leave me alone.

"Asher, go with me to get a coffee." Bray was suddenly standing in front of us, looking down at me. He knew I needed some space and Hannah didn't seem to get that.

I stood up and followed him out without a word to anyone around me. They'd all have to just understand. Small talk and words of courtesy were the last thing on my mind. Luke felt the same. He wasn't even in here for that very reason. He was keeping his distance from the crowd by staying away.

When we were far enough from everyone, Bray stopped walking. "I have no fucking clue where to get coffee. I was just thinking if I didn't get you out of there, you were gonna toss Hannah's hot ass out a window."

I wasn't going to go that far, but I was grateful he saved me. "I just need her to wake up like she's supposed to," I said staring out the window in front of us. Out there, the sun was still shining, the world was still turning, people were still living their lives unaware that others were locked away in here fighting for theirs. Their worlds hadn't stopped. Just ours.

I turned to Bray, "Scarlet came by yesterday morning. She was here when I woke up. She didn't stay because you and Brent would be coming. But she's close by. Waiting on news. Charlotte is keeping her updated."

Bray was silent for a couple minutes. I understood needing to be left alone with your thoughts to process it all. So I let him. We both stood there, with our arms crossed over our chests, our eyes on the world outside but not really seeing any of it. Both our minds were elsewhere.

"I'm not letting her go. Brent may hate me for life, but I can't let her go. She makes me sane. She understands and accepts me in a way no one else ever has. I can't let her go, Asher."

I knew he couldn't. I never expected it to be that easy.

"Seeing Dixie put into that helicopter, realizing that life can end so abruptly, just like dad's . . . I have to fight for her. Life could end for any of us at any moment."

I knew he hadn't meant to, but the image of Dixie being taken away caused a burning in my chest again. I just nodded in agreement. I had to catch my breath. I had to remember she was alive and I hadn't lost her.

"Shit. Didn't mean to upset you. You've gone fucking white."

"It's never going to be easy remembering those things."

Bray squeezed my shoulder. "No, it ain't," he agreed.

I started to say more when Charlotte's voice rang down the hallway, "She's awake."

My heart jumped in my chest. The long strides I took from where I had been standing with Bray to the room that Charlotte led me to were a blur. All I could think about was that Dixie's eyes were open. She was here. She was back.

When we reached the room, Luke was just walking out. He smiled at Charlotte. His eyes were full of joy while his cheeks were still damp from his tears. "She's asking for Asher."

I didn't wait for an invitation. I moved past both her parents and opened the door. Dixie looked so small on that bed, her skin pale and with all those wires connected to her body, but from the moment her eyes found mine, a smile curled on her lips.

I had prayed for days just to see that smile again, and just from seeing her there sitting up and awake, I started to cry.

"Asher," her voice was hoarse and soft. I moved toward her as my vision blurred from the tears and a sob tore from my chest. When I finally got to her, I laid my head in her lap and let the fear, relief, and all consuming love I felt for this woman break me further. Her hand touched my head and I just stayed there.

"I love you, too," she said. I smiled through the tears and lifted my head to see her. To take her in. To remind myself she was alive. We still had our forever ahead of us.

chapter
THIRTY-SEVEN

Luke Monroe

MY BABY GIRL was alive.

I stood outside her hospital room door while Asher Sutton sat by her side. The doctor gave us an update on the device they'd implanted on her heart to keep it beating. He explained how her life would be different.

"She will have regular doctor visits. She can eventually have regular exercise in her life. But moderate, nothing too strenuous. This is a hereditary condition so if she ever decides to have children, they'd have a 50/50 chance of having the same condition. That's a choice she will have to make. Do either of you have a history of any heart conditions in your family?"

I spoke, "Charlotte isn't her biological mother. And no, I've never had any issues. But her biological mother, she died of unknown causes. She had left us, so I didn't look into it. She hadn't been in our lives for five years at the time of her death." I hadn't wanted Dixie to know. I wanted to protect her from Millie, from all she'd done, all she was capable of doing. I didn't want Dixie to mourn a mother who wasn't worth it. She'd never loved Dixie. Millie had only loved herself.

The doctor nodded. "I'd be interested in finding out if it was heart related. There is a very high chance it was Long QT Syndrome and it just went undetected. It often does. Dixie is very lucky. I've said that to you before, but I need to stress to you just how lucky she is that you were there when she collapsed. You saved her life."

What if Charlotte hadn't been there? I couldn't think that way. She had been there and Dixie had lived.

"She will need to stay with us another week at least. Then we will need to put her in some physical therapy to ease her into things. Dixie is very strong and very determined. She has a life ahead of her now and the two of you to thank for it." He patted me on the back, then turned and left us.

"Will I ever stop asking myself what would have happened if I hadn't been there? What if I'd been outside? What if she'd been in her room and I hadn't heard her?" Charlotte was fighting her tears but slowly losing that battle.

I shook my head. "I don't know. I keep asking myself the same thing. And now I feel guilty for not looking into Millie's death and why it happened. Maybe if I'd known more and had Dixie checked on time, we would have been able to stop this from ever happening."

Charlotte wrapped her arms around one of mine. "We can't do that, Luke. She lived. She is okay. We were given this gift and we can't keep torturing ourselves with what ifs. We need to rejoice she is alive."

I kissed the top of her head. This woman had come into our lives when we needed her the most. She'd taught me to love again. To trust again. She'd given my daughter the kind of mother she deserved. She'd loved her like her own. And now she'd saved her life. My world before Charlotte had only one ray of light in it. My Dixie. But Charlotte gave it a rainbow.

"I love you, Charlotte Monroe. I became the luckiest man alive the day you walked into my life."

She tilted her head back and looked up at me. "You and Dixie gave me the first joy I'd ever had in life. I'm the lucky one."

I didn't argue. She was pretty damn lucky, too. We all were.

THIRTY-EIGHT

Asher Sutton

STEEL WAS STANDING alone outside the waiting room when I made my way back in there to give everyone an update, and to give Luke and Charlotte some time alone with Dixie. I stopped and waited for him to say what he was out here to say. This moment was coming. I knew he had things he needed to say. It was only fair. This had been hard on him, too. We both almost lost the girl we loved.

"She woke up and wanted you," he said simply.

It wasn't a question, just a simple statement.

"When she was taken away and we didn't know why or what was going on," he paused. "My first thoughts weren't of Dixie. They weren't of me. The first thing that ran through my head was that you wouldn't survive this. That was it. I was terrified, sure. The idea of Dixie . . . the whole damn thing was scary as hell. But my first thought was that you'd not make it through this if you lost her."

He paused and looked away from me. I watched as he

swallowed hard and took a deep breath. "I loved Dixie. Hell, I'll always care about her. But I love you more. You're my brother. It took that moment to show me how I felt about it all. I was worried about you. If I was meant to be with Dixie, I'd have been thinking of her. Like you were. You cared about nothing else but knowing she was alive. That she was going to make it. The rest of us were scared for her, too. But we were mostly focused on being strong for you."

I didn't know what to say to that. Instead of talking, I closed the space between us and hugged him. For forgiving me, for loving me, for understanding that Dixie was my heart. She had been for longer than even I realized.

"I want that, though. One day. What you have with her. I want to feel that way for someone. Maybe not tomorrow, or even next month. Hell, I might be good for a few years. But one day," he grinned as he said it.

"You will," I told him. "But expect it to be anything but easy."

"After what I've seen, what I've been through, I don't think love is meant to be easy. At least not the kind worth having."

He was right. Things that came easily were rarely worth keeping.

Heels clicking against the tile floor interrupted us. We both turned to see a familiar redhead. One that had made the twins' life anything but easy.

"Charlotte texted me that she's awake," Scarlet said. She looked thinner and had dark circles under her eyes. The light that I was used to seeing in her eyes was dimmed. Dixie would hate to see that. She'd worry about her.

"Yeah, I can take you to her room," I told her.

"Thank you."

"No problem. I know she wants to see you." Although I wished Scarlet looked a little less sad. For Dixie's sake.

"I'll go to the waiting room and, uh, manage things there," Steel said, meaning he'd keep Brent and Bray in there and away from Scarlet.

"Good idea."

Once he was gone, Scarlet said, "Looks like at least two of the Sutton boys have worked things out."

"We always do," I assured her. Because we did. We were brothers and shit may happen, but in the end, we were family.

"I want that for Brent and Bray," she sounded broken.

"They will be fine, eventually. But they can't get there if you're around." I knew that wasn't easy for her to hear, but it was the truth and she needed to know it.

She nodded in agreement.

chapter
THIRTY-NINE

Dixie Monroe

MY BEDROOM HAD been filled with flowers from friends and family. They were finally starting to wilt and die. The hospital room got too full so they'd brought most of them home throughout the week that I was there. Asher stayed the nights with me. He wouldn't leave my side and my dad said that if he or Mom stayed, Asher would just sleep in the waiting room on chairs. I begged them to let him stay with me. At least he had a sofa bed to sleep on in my room.

That week now seemed like a blur. I'd been home for over two weeks. My physical therapy was three times a week at a local place. Asher took me there and back to each appointment. We were together. We were no longer hiding.

When I'd first arrived home, it felt odd just even standing in that living room. I had basically died there. My heart had stopped beating. Thanks to my parents, it had only stopped for a few seconds before the paramedics arrived. But I had died in this very house and lived to tell about it.

Asher had stood behind me with his hand on my waist as I stared at the floor where I remembered everything going black. I didn't remember any white lights or angels sending me back to earth. I wasn't sure if that meant I hadn't died at all or if that white light thing was just a myth. But I knew my life would have ended had my family not been there.

Being back home felt good, though. Everything felt brighter. Life felt more precious. I didn't take anything for granted anymore. Asher came over after work every night and we had dinner together, watched television, and just laid out under the stars most nights. Being together was all that seemed to matter. We didn't talk about his plans for the future, but we both knew I wasn't going to Clemson now. Although the doctor said I could, I was scared. I knew in time I'd be brave again. I just needed some time to get used to this. I had enrolled at a junior college that I could drive to every day instead. Asher had one year left at Florida and being away from him was going to be difficult, but I would have him any way I could. I could survive the distance.

Tonight Asher had texted he'd be working late at the farm after he finished at the Feed and Seed. As much as I would miss him, I knew he'd given up all his free time for me. He had things he had to take care of and I couldn't be selfish. I took a shallow bath so that my stitches didn't get wet while I read a new book Mom had bought me. It helped pass the time.

When I stepped back into my room, I noticed there was a path of small envelopes leading to my window where my camera sat along with one last envelope leaning against it. I picked up the first one and opened it. Inside was a photo of me with Asher and Brent fishing with my dad at the lake. I was about nine years old. Smiling, I went to the next envelope and picked it up. It was a photo of me riding the handlebars of Asher's bike across the farm when I was eleven.

Picking up the third envelope, I was anxious to see the next picture. It was of me at thirteen, my cheeks pink from blushing as I stared at the photographer. I was sitting outside on the fence watching the horses. Asher had taken that photo. He'd been taking photos of the new horse Dad had brought to show the Knolls. But he had started taking pictures of me instead and I'd been so shy around him. And completely in love. It was obvious in the photo.

The fourth one was of us. Our first photo of us officially being together. Mom had taken it on my birthday. The birthday he had kissed me and given me the charm for my bracelet.

The fifth photo was of us at his Senior Prom. It was taken one week before he stopped speaking to me. I wasn't sure what the last envelope held. The prom photo had been the last one of us together. I opened it and found a note in it. "I'll see you at the lake. Bring the camera. We are due a new photo." Smiling, I put the note down and hurried to get dressed.

Pulling on a light blue sundress that fell just above my knees, I left my hair piled on top of my head because the summer nights were warm. It would still be sticky hot out there by the lake. I picked up the camera and headed downstairs.

Both my parents were watching the evening news. "I'm going to see Asher at the lake," I told them. "But someone had to let him in the house, so I guess y'all already know that."

Mom smiled. "Yes. He promised he'd have you back soon. Be careful."

"Be happy, baby girl. Just be happy," Dad added.

They were odd a bit lately. But then again, they'd been through a very traumatic experience. No one could blame them for not being themselves just yet. I hurried to the path that led to the lake, excited about being alone with Asher again. I knew we weren't going to be having sex just yet. I still had to discuss that with the doctor without my parents being present, but I could wait. I was happy just being alone with him.

I didn't see Asher's truck as I approached and wondered if I'd arrived before him. Maybe he had to take a shower first. I slowed my pace since I wasn't supposed to be running anyway and began to sit down on the grass when I heard something behind me. I turned around hoping it wasn't an animal out here in the darkness. And if it was one, I hoped it was the non-aggressive type.

Asher stepped out of the trees and into the moonlight. The silly smile on my face was unavoidable. Just seeing him made me feel that way.

"You've got the camera. Good," he said as he walked over to me and took it from me.

"I agree, but it's dark out here. We'll need the flash."

"Probably," was his only response.

He pressed a kiss to my lips and I sighed from the pleasure. Then he walked over to the trees and sat my camera down there.

"That's a nice camera to put in the grass," I pointed out.

He looked amused. "It won't be there long."

I was about to ask him what he was planning on doing with it when he stopped in front of me. "God, you're beautiful," he whispered. His hand caressed my left cheek as he looked into my eyes. "I thought for a moment I might not see this smile again. I wouldn't have survived without you." His words were spoken softly. As if he were thinking aloud. Allowing me into his thoughts. I started to speak, when he went down on one knee. I began to wonder if I was dreaming. Had I fallen asleep in the bathtub? This wasn't even a daydream or fantasy I had ever been brave enough to enjoy because I never believed it would be mine.

He held out an ice blue velvet box and opened it. Inside was the most perfect ring in the world. I wasn't sure what it looked like exactly because my eyes were filling with tears and blurring my vision, but Asher was holding it and he was on one knee and that made it perfect. It could be from a gumball machine for all I cared.

"I've loved you most of my life. Without you, my world has no laughter. No sunshine. No joy. You bring all that when you smile. I can't do life without you. I tried. I need you, Dixie Monroe. I need you today and for the rest of our lives. Will you—"

"Yes!" I said on a sob, not waiting for him to even finish. "Yes, yes, yes!" I chanted. Then I paused. He had one year of college left. He'd be leaving soon. I wouldn't let him give that up for me. Not because he feared losing me. He would never lose me.

"But you've got college."

"So do you," he replied. "And it's just a year for me and we've got our entire lives together."

He was right. We had forever. I wasn't dying anytime soon. I had to live so I'd get this life with Asher I'd always wanted. "Yes! It's still yes," I said, wiping at the tears streaming down my face.

He stood up and pulled me into his arms before sliding the ring on my finger. It wasn't from a gumball machine. It was a perfect teardrop shaped diamond.

A flash went off in the darkness causing me to jump. I blinked trying to regain my vision. Once I could focus again, I saw Asher smiling, his gaze toward the trees. I turned to see Brent, Bray, Dallas and Steel walking out of the woods. They all looked happy. Even Steel.

"It's about damn time you married into this family. You've been trying to get in it since you could walk," Bray said holding the camera and taking another shot.

I looked from them up to Asher. "I guess you Sutton boys don't do anything alone."

He shrugged. "We do some things. Just not the important things. And it doesn't get any more important than this."

A few more pictures were snapped as I laughed and wrapped my arms around him.

Each brother came up to me and hugged me before leaving. Each one having something to say in my ear just for me to hear. I knew Asher would ask me later what they said. And I would tell him.

When it was Steel's turn, he whispered, "It's okay now. I get it. We both knew it was always him." It was bittersweet. I did care for Steel. He'd come along when I needed someone. He gave me some happiness during a dark time. I'd always love him for that.

After the last brother walked back into the woods, Asher brought my ringed finger to his mouth and kissed it. "Hard to believe this is real."

I couldn't agree more. "We went through a lot to get to this point but, Asher, I don't want this to be because you thought you were going to lose me. I want you to be ready for this." I feared that my almost death had made him move too fast on something too important to rush. I knew what I had just been through was the reason Steel was so accepting. When faced with death, you see the world differently.

"The day I kissed you outside my truck when you were fifteen, I started planning this moment. I've known you were my one since then, Dix. Even when I thought it was impossible. Your face . . . it was all I saw. All I'll *ever* see."

And his would be the only one for me.

ACKNOWLEDGEMENTS

WHEN I WRITE a book it isn't just me involved. It takes many for my words to make it to publication.

Jack Britton Sullivan "Britt" aka "baby daddy"- he edits it all. I listen to his advice and he spends hours every day cleaning my writing up. Thank you!

Murphy Rae Indie Solutions- this cover could not be more perfect. Thank you!

Christine Borgford- makes my formatting awesome and pretty. I always love how she makes my stories look. Thank you!

Jane Dystel and Lauren Abramo- y'all support me no matter how I'm publishing: Traditional or self publishing. Thank you both! I am so very lucky to have a wonderful literary agency standing behind me.

Danielle Lagasse, Vicci Kaighan and Abbi's Army- these women are what keep me going on days I think I can't. When I'm down they remind me I have readers who can't wait for my next book. They promote me, share my books with others, and are all around the best street team ever.

Monica Tucker and Stefanie Burgett- I couldn't get through the day without these two. They handle the side of things I don't have time to do. I write, they do the rest. Thank you ladies!

ABBI GLINES

ABBI GLINES IS a #1 New York Times, USA Today, and Wall Street Journal bestselling author of the Rosemary Beach, Sea Breeze, Vincent Boys, Existence, and The Field Party Series . She never cooks unless baking during the Christmas holiday counts. She believes in ghosts and has a habit of asking people if their house is haunted before she goes in it. She drinks afternoon tea because she wants to be British but alas she was born in Alabama. When asked how many books she has written she has to stop and count on her fingers. When she's not locked away writing, she is reading, shopping (major shoe and purse addiction), sneaking off to the movies alone, and listening to the drama in her teenagers lives while making mental notes on the good stuff to use later. Don't judge.

You can connect with Abbi online in several different ways. She uses social media to procrastinate.

www.abbiglines.com
www.facebook.com/abbiglinesauthor
twitter.com/AbbiGlines
www.instagram.com/abbiglines
www.pinterest.com/abbiglines

books by
ABBI GLINES

ROSEMARY BEACH SERIES
Fallen Too Far
Never Too Far
Forever Too Far
Rush Too Far
Twisted Perfection
Simple Perfection
Take A Chance
One More Chance
You We're Mine
Kiro's Emily
When I'm Gone
When You're Back
The Best Goodbye
Up In Flames

SEA BREEZE SERIES
Breathe
Because of Low
While It Lasts
Just For Now
Sometimes It Lasts
Misbehaving
Bad For You
Hold On Tight
Until The End

SEA BREEZE MEETS ROSEMARY BEACH
Like A Memory

THE FIELD PARTY SERIES
Until Friday Night
Under the Lights
After the Game (Coming August 22, 2017)

ONCE SHE DREAMED
Once She Dreamed (Part 1)
Once She Dreamed (Part 2)

THE VINCENT BOYS SERIES
The Vincent Boys
The Vincent Brothers

EXISTENCE TRILOGY
Existence (Book 1)
Predestined (Book 2)
Leif (Book 2.5)
Ceaseless (Book 3)

Made in the USA
Columbia, SC
17 February 2019